KT-442-746

Dear Reader

I like a peaceful life. Although I'm prepared to argue for things I feel strongly about, I won't go out to pick a fight with anyone. So in many ways it went against the grain to write about Nick and Abby, who don't seem to agree on anything and have little hesitation in telling each other so.

As they battled their way through the pages, though, I grew to love them. Their passion. Their refusal to give up when many would have just shrugged and walked away. They're both fighters and, although they can't see it, that's one of the many reasons they should be together.

Thank you for reading Nick and Abby's story. I hope you enjoy it. I'm always delighted to hear from readers, and you can email me via my website, which is at: www.annieclaydon.com

Annie

Cursed from an early age with a poor sense of direction and a propensity to read, **Annie Claydon** spent much of her childhood lost in books. After completing her degree in English Literature, she indulged her love of romantic fiction and spent a long, hot summer writing a book of her own. It was duly rejected and life took over, with a series of U-turns leading in the unlikely direction of a career in computing and information technology. The lure of the printed page proved too much to bear, though, and she now has the perfect outlet for the stories which have always run through her head, writing Medical Romance™ for Mills and Boon. Living in London, a city where getting lost can be a joy, she has no regrets in having taken her time in working her way back to the place that she started from.

THE DOCTOR MEETS HER MATCH

BY
ANNIE CLAYDON

All the characters in this book have no existence outside the imagination of the author, and have no relation whatsoever to anyone bearing the same name or names. They are not even distantly inspired by any individual known or unknown to the author, and all the incidents are pure invention.

All Rights Reserved including the right of reproduction in whole or in part in any form. This edition is published by arrangement with Harlequin Enterprises II BV/S.à.r.l. The text of this publication or any part thereof may not be reproduced or transmitted in any form or by any means, electronic or mechanical, including photocopying, recording, storage in an information retrieval system, or otherwise, without the written permission of the publisher.

® and TM are trademarks owned and used by the trademark owner and/or its licensee. Trademarks marked with ® are registered with the United Kingdom Patent Office and/or the Office for Harmonisation in the Internal Market and in other countries.

First published in Great Britain 2012
by Mills & Boon, an imprint of Harlequin (UK) Limited.
Large Print edition 2013
Harlequin (UK) Limited, Eton House,
18-24 Paradise Road, Richmond, Surrey TW9 1SR

© Annie Claydon 2012

ISBN: 978 0 263 23100 7

Harlequin (UK) policy is to use papers that are natural, renewable and recyclable products and made from wood grown in sustainable forests. The logging and manufacturing process conform to the legal environmental regulations of the country of origin.

Printed and bound in Great Britain
by CPI Antony Rowe, Chippenham, Wiltshire

Recent titles by Annie Claydon:

DOCTOR ON HER DOORSTEP
ALL SHE WANTS FOR CHRISTMAS

**These books are also available in
eBook format from www.millsandboon.co.uk**

To Kath.
For the past, the present and the future.

CHAPTER ONE

ABBY had five seconds to recover from the shock of seeing Nick again. Five heartbeats before his heavy eyelids fluttered open and he focussed on her. She could have done with ten at the very least.

The working clamour of the A and E department receded to the very edge of her consciousness. There was only Nick now, propped up on a trolley, one leg free of the cellular blanket that covered him, and his eyes dull with pain.

Somehow she got her legs to work and she took two steps forward into the cubicle and pulled the curtain shut behind her. Glancing at the A and E notes in the vain hope that somewhere there was another fireman with trauma to the knee who she was really supposed to be examining, she saw his name printed at the top. Nick Hunter. How on earth could she have missed that?

'Abby?'

'Nick.' This was no good. She should be calm, in control, not red faced and staring at him as if she'd just seen a ghost. She wrenched her gaze from his dark, suede-soft eyes. 'I've been called down from Orthopaedics to see you. I gather you've been waiting a while.'

'They're pretty busy with the guy I pulled out of that car. How is he? He didn't look good…'

'They're working on him.' Abby almost snapped at him, and she took a deep breath and started again. 'I'll see if I can find out for you. But first we need to get you sorted out.'

'Okay. Thanks.' He was watching her intently. Waiting for her next move.

What on earth *was* her next move? Nick wasn't just a patient, he was a…what? Not a friend any more. He'd seen to that when he'd cut off all contact with her six months ago, not returning her calls and disappearing out of her life like a puff of smoke. He wasn't a lover. He'd never been that, even if at one time Abby had wanted it, more than she now cared to admit.

He was a guy that she'd met at the swimming

pool, got to know, along with the group he swam with, and then gone on a couple of casual dates with. That was all. Hardly a close personal relationship, although at the time it had felt a lot like it.

All the same, she had to put this onto a professional footing. Keep it there. 'Right, then. A and E is very busy tonight and I've been called to see you as my speciality is orthopaedics...' She licked her lips. He knew all that. 'So, are you happy for me to examine you?'

He shrugged and Abby's stomach twisted. She'd obviously made a lot more of this than it actually was. 'Of course...'

'Because I can get another doctor...' Easier said than done at seven o' clock on a Friday evening, when everyone else was either busy or had gone home, but she'd deal with that if she came to it. 'We know each other, Nick. If you have any objection to me examining and treating you then you should say so now. It's quite okay...'

'I'd rather it was you, Abby.' His gaze seemed to soften. 'You're better qualified than anyone here to treat a knee injury, and from the looks of it I'll have to wait a while to see anyone else. I'm fine with it…as long as you are?'

He shot her a look that made her heart hurt. But she'd been down that road before and Abby wasn't going to be seduced by his smile again. If he could get past what had happened, so should she. It had probably meant nothing to him anyway.

She concentrated on the facts. Act always in the patient's best interests. Right now, it was clearly not in Nick's best interests to wait another three hours for treatment, just because of what had gone on in her head six months ago. Nothing even remotely inappropriate had happened. She had to pull herself together and get on with her job. 'So it's just your knee, then. Nothing else?'

'Just my knee. I think I've twisted it badly.'

'How did it happen? You were underneath the car when you did it or did you fall?'

'No, the frame of the car buckled as I was crawling back out from underneath it. Caught my knee here.' He indicated an angry red haematoma.

'Did you twist the leg at all?' Keep it on this

level. Details of his injury. His medical condition. They were a welcome barrier, standing between a woman and the man who had hurt her.

He grinned. 'Probably. I was concentrating on moving as fast as I could at that point.'

Unwanted respect flared in Abby's chest. Crawling into the tangled remains of a car to get someone out of the wreckage took a special kind of courage. 'Okay, let me take a look at it. Tell me if I'm hurting you.'

Pulling a pair of surgical gloves from the dispenser, she gently probed the swelling around the knee, lifting it slightly to check the movement of the joint. His sharp intake of breath stopped her, and when she swung round she could see his fingers gripped tightly around the bars at the side of the bed.

'I said tell me if it hurts, Nick. I'm not a mind reader.'

'Right. Yeah, it hurts.'

'And this?'

'Yes.'

'Okay. What's this scar, here? It looks as if you've had some surgery.'

'I had an operation on the knee four years ago to repair torn cartilage.'

'How did you do that?'

He managed to muster a grin and the temperature in the cubicle shot back up suddenly. 'Put my foot through a floorboard in a burnt out building. I twisted the knee as I fell.' Even here, even now, he was the best-looking man Abby had ever seen. Dark brown hair, cut short so that it spiked haphazardly when he ran his hand through it. A short, deep scar, running through his eyebrow, which was the one asymmetric feature of an otherwise stunningly handsome face.

'I'll see if I can find a record of that on our system. The operation was done here?'

He nodded, his lips quirking downwards then pressing together in a thin line.

'Right, then.' She scanned the notes quickly. 'It says here that you were offered pain control in the ambulance and you turned it down. Would you like something now?'

'No. I'm fine, thanks.'

He didn't need to pretend he wasn't in pain. She

was a doctor, not a woman he needed to impress. 'On a scale of one to ten...'

'About one and a quarter.' He didn't even let her finish.

'Really?' She raised an eyebrow to make it clear that she didn't believe him for a minute, and he ignored her. Abby had seen that kind of flat-out denial before but it was puzzling coming from Nick. She'd get back to that one later.

'Okay, let me know if you change your mind and I can give you something that will make you much more comfortable.' He nodded almost imperceptibly. 'I'm going to send you for some X-rays, and I'll come back and see you again when I've reviewed them.' That would give Abby at least half an hour to gather her wits. Maybe more. Perhaps the next time she laid eyes on him, she'd be able to retain her composure a little better.

'Thanks.' He hesitated, as if something was bothering him. 'I hope I'm not keeping you from going home. It must be gone seven o'clock.'

Twenty past. The charge nurse from A and E had called her just as she'd finished catching up on the week's paperwork and had been about to leave. 'Not a problem. That's what I'm here for.' It seemed that finally, despite all Abby's promises to herself, she was going to be spending one more evening in Nick's company.

By the time Nick's X-rays were back, Abby had already found his notes on the computer and read them. And it gave her no pleasure whatsoever to find he was wrong. She took a deep breath before she made her way back to his bedside to deliver the bad news.

'Hey, there.' His smile was too broad. Slightly brittle.

'How are you doing?'

'Thought you might be able to tell me.' He nodded at the large manila folder she carried.

'Yeah.' Abby sat down by his bedside. Whatever she felt about his behaviour towards her, she had to give him credit for his resilience. She knew how much pain he must be in, and it was searing through her. That trick of being able to insulate yourself from a patient's pain didn't seem to be working so well for her at the moment.

'What's the verdict, then?'

'The X-rays show a hairline crack on your patella.'

He stared at her as if he didn't understand, or perhaps he just wasn't taking her word for it. Abby drew one of the X-rays out of the folder, holding it up to the strip light above his head. 'Here, can you see?'

He shifted closer to her to look, and reached up, steadying her hand with his. His touch was still electric. The soft brush of his fingers against her wrist made the hairs on the back of her neck stand up. 'I can't see anything.'

'Right there.' She indicated the line of the fracture, trying to ignore the fact that she was leaning over him. That she would be able to hear his heartbeat if she got any closer. 'The good news is that it's not displaced, so it should heal relatively quickly.'

'I see.' He squinted at the area she had indicated. 'It doesn't look too bad, then?'

Abby bit her tongue. Asking him whether that statement was based on medical knowledge or wishful thinking probably wasn't appropriate. Neither was enjoying leaning over him. At the swimming pool it had been pretty much impossible not to notice Nick's beautiful physique. Here it was irrelevant.

She straightened quickly. 'Well, a fractured patella is never good. But it could have been a lot worse. From the looks of your knee there may well be some other damage, though, and I'm ordering an MRI scan to see what's happening with the cartilage and to get a better view of the fracture.'

'But if that's okay…?' He sat up straight on the trolley, as if their business was now finished and he could go. Abby fixed him with the sternest glare she could muster. This was her territory and she was in charge.

'There's still the matter of the crack on your patella. You're going to need to rest it and wear a brace for four to six weeks.'

He ran his hand back through his hair in a gesture of frustration. 'Four weeks?'

'Four to six weeks. That's pretty much how long a bone takes to mend.' Abby bit her lip. Enough sarcasm. He was in pain here, and she knew how much Nick loved his job. The least she could do was show him a bit of understanding. 'I'm sorry, but you won't be fit enough to go back to work for a while.'

'How long?'

'I can't tell for sure at this point. I'm going to refer you on for an early appointment with a colleague who specialises in injuries of this kind. By the time you see him, we should have managed to get some of this swelling down and the MRI results will be available. He'll be able to tell you much more.'

'Yes. Of course.' He took a deep breath. 'Thanks for everything, Abby. Can I go now?'

He really didn't want to be around her. She could tell from the way he was focussing past her, on something just over her right shoulder. He'd do anything but look her in the eye.

That was fine. Abby didn't much want to be around Nick either but that wasn't the point of this particular exercise. She was a doctor and he was a patient. If she reminded herself of that enough times, she'd get it in the end. 'Not yet. I need to sort out a suitable knee brace for you, along with some painkillers and anti-inflammatory drugs.' She fixed him with a stern look. 'Stay there, I'll be back shortly.'

Abby didn't wait for his answer. Making for the curtain, which covered the entrance to the cubicle, she yanked it firmly closed and caught the charge nurse's eye. If he attempted to run out on her this time, he'd find that the A and E staff were more than a match for him.

Abby was in a class all of her own when she did stern. Nick tried not to think about that, and concentrated on all the reasons why continuing their relationship had been a seriously bad idea. Why he'd been right to walk away before the shimmer in her light blue eyes, the little quirk of her mouth when she'd smiled, had pulled him spiralling out of control. Even now it was tough work to resist her.

Not that she was doing a great deal of smiling this evening. She didn't seem to be having much trouble with resisting him either. She'd drawn back so quickly when he'd touched her that he'd wondered whether an apology was in order. Common sense was yet another thing he had to award her ten out of ten for.

He pulled himself up into a sitting position and swung his good leg over the edge of the trolley. So far so good. Kind of. He gripped his injured leg and tried to move it and pain seared from his calf to his thigh. Not such a good idea. Nick reached for his jacket, which was over the back of the chair where his clothes were folded, managing to pull his phone from the pocket with the tips of his fingers.

When he switched it on, there were two missed calls, and a text. *Off duty in ten. Be there in half an hour.* Nick looked at his watch. Sam would be arriving in fifteen minutes and, with any luck, by that time Nick would be dressed and ready to go.

'It'll be a lot easier with this. And you're supposed to keep that switched off.'

Nick's gaze jerked upwards from the small screen on his phone and found Abby's half-amused grimace. 'What will?'

'Your escape.' She shrugged, walking to his bedside and propping the pair of elbow crutches she carried against the chair. 'Swing your leg back onto the bed while I sort this knee brace out.'

She fiddled for a while with the ugly-looking

contraption, rolling her eyes and grinning when the Velcro straps tangled themselves together and stuck fast. Nick added *kindness* to the list of her virtues. Even though he'd treated her badly, there was no trace of reproach in her attitude towards him.

'Just relax and let me move your leg. I'll try not to hurt you too much.' She gently took hold of his leg and Nick braced himself for the pain, letting out an involuntary breath when it wasn't half as bad as when he'd tried to move it himself.

'There.' She carefully fastened the brace and stood back, reviewing her handiwork. 'How does that feel?'

'Better. Thanks, it feels much better with the support.' Nick had been concentrating on the gentle warmth of her fingers, the way her corn-coloured plait of hair threatened to slip forward over her shoulder when she bent forward. Her scent, which seemed to be more than just the astringent, soapy smell of the other doctors and nurses here. They were far more potent than the drugs he'd refused.

'Good. I've set it at an angle to keep your knee

bent, and you should leave it like that until you see my colleague. Don't put any weight on the leg for the time being, and it'll help if you use cushions to support it when you're sitting or lying down.' She paused, seemingly deep in thought. 'Let's see if we can't get you back onto your feet.'

At last! Nick sat up and she helped him swing his leg over the side of the trolley. 'Lean on my shoulder if you need to.'

He couldn't think of anything more comforting at that moment than to take advantage of her offer. 'Thanks, but I'm okay.' Levering himself upwards with his arms, he put one foot to the floor and stood up slowly.

'Good. That's good.' She reached for the crutches, extending one to almost its full height, and gave it to him. 'Yes, that looks about right.' She adjusted the other and suddenly Nick was free. Able to move around again.

'Walk up and down a bit.' She watched carefully as he took a few tentative steps, leaning on the crutches, and nodded in approval. 'That looks fine. Is it comfortable?'

'Yes. The brace is a little tight.'

'It needs to be. As the swelling goes down, you should tighten it a little so it feels snug. Without cutting off the circulation to your foot, that is.' A sudden grin, which was quashed almost immediately, made Nick's head swim slightly. His own body was producing powerful endorphins in response to that lopsided, shining smile of hers, and he could do nothing to stop it.

'Thanks. Can I get dressed now?'

The words had an almost instant effect on her. She backed away. 'Do you need someone to help you? I can send someone in.'

'I'm fine.' Nick grinned to himself as she disappeared out of the cubicle. Maybe he should have thought of that one sooner.

The A and E nurse had cut the leg of his trousers to get them off and it was easy enough to slip them back on again. Discarding the flimsy hospital gown and pulling on his shirt, Nick struggled with getting his sock onto his injured leg and decided to carry his boot. A quick phone call elicited the information that Sam was outside, trying to find a parking space.

'Right.' The curtain had twitched slightly, indicating that she'd checked first to make sure he was dressed, before she breezed back into his cubicle. 'I've got a leaflet here, to give you some guidelines on how to manage the leg.' She proffered a printed sheet and Nick took it. Next to one of the items she had drawn a star and written a few notes. Even her handwriting was bewitching. Nick wondered briefly whether it was possible to be seduced by someone's handwriting, before folding the sheet and putting it into his jacket pocket.

'Thanks. I appreciate all you've done, Abby.' It was time for him to leave. Before she got around to the prescription she held in her hand. Before he got too used to the light that seemed to shine from her and gravitated towards it, like a moth whose wings had already been burned by the flame.

'Oh, no, you don't.' She was quicker than he was at the moment, and blocked his path. 'Sit down for a moment. I've had a colleague write you a prescription for something to control your pain.'

She was keeping him well and truly at arm's

length. Somehow the fact that she'd got someone else to write the prescription rankled more
than anything. As if she was trying to wipe him
from every corner of her life. Nick wondered if
she'd been hurt as badly as he had by what had
happened between them.

'I don't need it.' The words sounded harsh and
ungrateful. 'Thanks, Abby, but I don't want it.
Sam'll be here to pick me up any minute.'

'Sam!' She jumped like a startled fawn, flushing slightly. She did remember, then. The leisurely Sunday morning breakfasts after training
when Sam and the half-dozen others at the table
had faded into blurred insignificance, and there
had only been Nick and Abby. The reckless slide
into dinner and the cinema. He'd fallen for her
hard and fast, before sanity had taken hold and
convinced him to draw back.

She pulled herself together with impressive
speed. 'He'll have to wait, then, we're not finished yet. You should have something to control the pain and bring the inflammation down.
I really can't recommend that you be discharged
without it...'

'Then I'll discharge myself.'

The conversation had finally degenerated into a game of chicken. Whose nerve was going to break first. In the end, no one broke. Sam's light touch on Abby's shoulder made her jump again and she whirled round to face him.

'Abby. Where have you been? Long time no see...' Nick directed his most ferocious glare in Sam's direction and Sam got the message. 'So how's he doing, then?'

She pursed her lips as if she was considering the question and Nick broke in. 'We're done here.'

'Really?' Sam gave Abby a quizzical look and she frowned.

'No. Not really. Nick...'

In between him and Sam, she suddenly looked small. Vulnerable. Staring up at them with what looked like frightened defiance in her eyes. The urge to protect her leaked into Nick's aching bones, almost before he realised that the only thing Abby needed protecting from was him.

He slid past her, brushing against her as he went. 'I'm sorry.' He was sorry for everything. The way he'd left her without a word of explanation six months ago. How he was leaving things between them now. But if she knew his reasons she'd be the first to want him gone. 'Thanks for all you've done.'

The words stuck in his throat because he knew they weren't enough. But they were all he could give her and he lunged forward on his crutches. He heard her exclamation of frustration behind him and Nick made for the exit doors without looking back.

CHAPTER TWO

SAM had given her a grinning shrug and followed Nick, jogging to catch up with him. Abby didn't stop to watch them go. She did what she had schooled herself to do as a teenager and which now came as second nature to her. If someone hurts you, don't go running after them. Turn away. Be strong.

'How did that go?' She was concentrating hard on Not Caring and the voice at her elbow made her jump.

'Michael. I didn't see you there.'

'Penny for them?' Michael Gibson, the A and E doctor who would have seen Nick had he not been with a more urgent patient, was standing beside her.

'Not worth it.' She held the prescription form up for Michael to see. 'He didn't take it.'

'No? Why not?'

'I don't know. He just said that he didn't need it. Stayed long enough for an X-ray and for me to give him a diagnosis and then as soon as I let him get his hands on a pair of crutches he was off. I couldn't stop him.'

'What were you thinking of doing? Handcuffing him to the bed?'

Don't say things like that, Michael. You'll give a girl ideas. 'I...I just can't help thinking that he would have taken it from someone else.'

Michael sighed. 'Look, Abs. You asked him if he was okay with you treating him, you ran everything past me. Aren't you overthinking this a bit? People make decisions about what level of treatment they're going to take from us all the time.'

'I guess so.' Abby wasn't convinced. She wouldn't lay the blame on Nick when she should be shouldering it herself. His decision must have been something to do with her.

Michael looked at his watch. 'Can you do me a favour and write up the notes, then sort out a referral?'

'Of course. You get on. I'll put him on the list

for an early MRI scan and get him an appointment up in Orthopaedics.' Abby grinned. 'With someone else, who might be able to talk some sense into him.'

'Don't sweat it so much, Abby.' The charge nurse had caught Michael's eye and he was already turning to see his next patient for the evening. 'All we can do is our best.'

She'd spent half the night considering that rationally, and the other half beating her head against an imaginary brick wall, which might just as well have been real from the way her head was throbbing this morning. The only thing that Abby was sure of was that she'd messed up somehow and that she had to put it right.

Something had made him act that way. He was perfectly at liberty to walk out on her as a woman and she was at liberty to hate him for it. But if a little of the past had leaked through into her attitude towards Nick last night and made him refuse medical treatment he needed, that was unforgivable. Whatever Michael had said, she had to put it right.

Not giving herself time to change her mind, Abby got out of the car, marched quickly up the front path and pressed the doorbell. No one answered. She was about to turn and walk away when a bump from inside the house told her that Nick hadn't gone out. She thumbed the doorbell again, this time letting it ring insistently.

'Okay! Give me a minute…' The door was flung open and Nick froze.

'Hello.' She was expecting to see him this time, but that didn't seem to lessen the shock all that much.

'Hi…Abby.' He had the presence of mind not to say it, but his eyes demanded an answer. *What are you doing here?*

'I came to see how you were.' Her hands were shaking but her lips were smiling. Not too much. Professional.

'You didn't need to. I'm fine. Thanks.' Nick was leaning on the crutches she'd given him, his loose sweatpants stretched over the bulky brace. That was something. At least he hadn't taken it off and thrown it away as soon as he'd got home.

'I think we have a little unfinished business, Nick.'

He pressed his lips together. 'I know. I should have called you, it was unforgivable...'

'Not that.' Abby had spent some time convincing herself that the events of six months ago were all water under the bridge, and she wasn't going to let Nick bring it up now. 'I mean from last night. You left before I had a chance to finish...' She stopped, flushing. Her voice sounded like a pathetic, childish whine, as if she was begging for his attention.

Understanding flickered in his eyes. His warmth curled around her senses and just as Abby's knees began to liquefy her defences clicked in. This man was not going to see her vulnerable. Not again.

'I left because I was done. It was nothing to do with you.'

Abby straightened herself. 'What was it to do with?'

'It's none of your business, Abby...' He seemed to be about to say more but stopped himself. 'Look, as I said, it's really good of you to come here and I want to thank you for everything you've done. But you'll have to excuse me.'

She wasn't giving up without a fight. The door was closing, and there were only two things that Abby could think of to do. She wasn't quite angry enough to punch him—not yet, anyway—so she stuck her foot in the doorway, bracing herself for the blow of the door as he tried to close it.

It didn't come. There was nothing wrong with Nick's reflexes and he whipped the door back open before it hit her foot. 'Abby...' His gaze met hers, dark and full of pain, and concern for him grated across her nerve endings. There was no point in that. Nick wasn't the type to accept sympathy. She faced him down, and saw a flare of what might have been tenderness.

Wordlessly he stepped back from the doorway, turned, and made his way back along the hall, leaving the door open behind him. It wasn't the most cordial of invitations she'd ever received but Abby followed him, closing the door behind her.

'Can I get you some coffee?' He had led her through to the kitchen, a large, bright room where the house had been extended at the back. Indicating that she should sit down at the sturdy wooden table, he swung across to the counter and reached up into a cupboard for a tin of coffee beans.

'Thanks.' Abby sat down. Making coffee and drinking it would take at least ten minutes. She could use that time.

'Toast?' The room smelled of fresh bread and there was a loaf, just out of the breadmaker, on the countertop.

'Thanks. I didn't have breakfast this morning.' Fifteen minutes. Even better. Time enough to sort this out and then get out of there.

Nick didn't turn to face her and Abby sat down. Without a word, he ground the coffee beans and switched the coffee machine on, then shifted awkwardly across to cut the bread, leaning one of his crutches against the sink.

'Here, let me help you.'

'I can manage.'

She dropped back down into her chair. He seemed to be managing not to look at her as well. It occurred to Abby that the offer of coffee hadn't been intended as hospitality as much as an excuse not to sit down and talk to her.

Finally he was done. He'd made tea for himself, and Abby jumped up to ferry the cups and plates to the table, while Nick lowered himself into a chair.

'We don't need to argue about this.' He gave her a persuasive grin. 'We could just agree to differ and enjoy our breakfast.'

Nick's charm didn't work on her any more. Much. 'Or we could talk about why I think it's important that you take the medication you've been offered. I'm here to help you. As a friend, Nick.' 'Friends' was dangerous territory. But being his doctor was becoming more inappropriate by the minute, and that was the only other excuse she had to be there.

His lips twitched. 'And you think that I'm not helping myself?'

'From where I'm sitting, that's how it looks.' Abby took a sip of her coffee.

'I guess it might.' The words were almost a challenge.

'It does, Nick. Pain control isn't just about making things easier for you. With an injury like this, it's important that you give your body a chance to heal. That means being able to sleep and move around gently. You need to get some of that swelling around your knee down as well.'

'I've been putting ice packs on it. The swelling's down from yesterday.'

'That's better than nothing. How much sleep did you get last night?'

Nick didn't answer. He didn't need to. The dark hollows beneath his eyes and the stiffness of his movements attested to how little he'd slept and how much he was hurting right now. Abby could strike the suspicion of him having decided to self-medicate from the list of possibilities.

'Did you take analgesics the last time you hurt your knee?' Abby could have looked that up on the hospital's computer system after he'd left, but she'd baulked at that.

He nodded. Another couple of options to strike off the list. Whatever his reason was, it must be something that had happened in the four years, since his last injury. 'Are you saying you had an adverse reaction to one of the drugs?'

'No. I'm saying that I don't want the drugs now.'

'Nick, if you don't want to tell me what the

problem is, that's fine. But you wouldn't let me do my best for you last night, and I can tell you now that's not the way that I work and it's not the way the doctor I've referred you to works either.' Abby could feel the colour rising in her cheeks, and checked herself.

Something bloomed in his eyes, which looked suspiciously like respect, and Abby ignored the answering quiver in the pit of her stomach. She didn't need Nick's respect, she just needed him to see the logic of what she was trying to tell him.

'Since you put it that way…' He seemed lost in thought for a moment and then jerked his head up to face her, his stare daring her to look away. 'I'm a drug addict.'

His message was clear. Get back. Stay back. Nick knew that Abby was not stupid. She had to understand it and the only other explanation was that she was planning on ignoring it.

'Okay. What kind of drugs?' She was doing a fairly good job of staring him down. There was barely a flicker at the corner of her eye.

'Painkillers. The kind that were prescribed for me. And others that weren't.'

'But you're clean now.'

'What makes you think that?' He'd never be truly clean.

'If you were still taking opiate drugs, for whatever purpose, maybe you would have slept a little better last night.'

'Yeah. Fair enough.' It would take more than just staying off the drugs to make him whole, but Nick was done with admitting things. That was all she needed to know. He reached for his keys, which were sitting at the far end of the table where he'd dumped them last night, and showed her the small engraved disc that served as a key fob.

She leaned forward to focus on the letters, alongside a logo with a set of initials. 'IK. What's that?'

'Stands for one thousand days. In that time I haven't had as much as an aspirin or a cup of coffee.' Her gaze flicked involuntarily towards the cup of herbal tea in front of him, and Nick wondered how much of this she had already worked out for herself. 'I earned this six months ago, and I'm not giving it up for anything.'

'Your support group asks that you give up everything? Aspirin, coffee...?'

'No. That's what I require of myself.'

She sucked in a deep breath, seeming to relax slightly as she exhaled. 'I'd like to help, Nick. If you'll let me.'

She'd disarmed him completely. Maybe it was the way that sunlight from the window became entangled in her hair and couldn't break free. Maybe her steady, blue gaze, which held the promise of both cornflowers and steel. 'What do you suggest?'

Nick was expecting one, maybe two platitudes about not overstepping the mark again and a lecture on how effective ice-packs could be. Then she could do the sensible thing and wash her hands of him.

Instead, she drew a pad from her handbag, turned to a page of scribbled notes, asked questions and made some more notes. Then she produced a bundle of printed pages from the internet, selecting some for him to look at, which left Nick in little doubt that she had come prepared for almost every eventuality, including the one which he had just admitted to. He hadn't thought that Abby was such a force to be reckoned with.

'What do you think, then?'

Nick had no idea what he thought. He'd heard everything she'd said, but the bulk of his attention had been concentrated on the soft curl of her eyelashes. On trying to resist the impulse to reach out and touch the few golden strands of hair that strayed across her cheek, aware that he could so easily become trapped. 'Sounds logical.'

She rolled her eyes, twisting her head to one side in a shimmer of liquid light, and he almost choked on his tea. 'It's obviously logical. But how do you feel about it?'

'Okay, then.' There wasn't much option other than the truth, not with Abby. 'I'd rather stick pins in my eyes.'

'Fair enough, but can you do it?'

'Stick pins in my eyes? I'd rather not.'

She gifted him with a glare that made his stomach tighten. 'Stop messing around, Nick. Will you do this?' She tapped the list she'd made with her pen.

A visit to a pain clinic, specialising in drug-free therapies, which Abby had assured him was among the best in its field. Taking the clinic's advice on non-opiate painkillers and anti-inflammatory drugs. Coming clean with the orthopaedic surgeon that Abby had already arranged for Nick to see at the hospital, and having him work with the clinic to provide what she termed as 'joined-up' care.

'I can do it.' This would be harder than dealing with the constant, throbbing pain in his knee but Nick saw the sense in it. It was his best chance of being able to get back on his feet again any time soon.

'So I'll call the pain clinic and try to get you an emergency appointment for this afternoon.'

'I'm not a child. I can make a phone call.' The thought that maybe she didn't trust him hurt more than it should have. What reason had he ever given her to trust him?

'I know. But this is supposed to be the exact opposite of what you did before. You take help. You don't self-medicate. You follow an agreed plan and you keep everyone informed and in touch with what's happening.'

She grinned persuasively at him. He'd missed her smile. 'If something was on fire, I'd be letting *you* take charge.'

'I have a box of matches in the drawer over there…' He held his hands up as she shot him a look of such ferocity that laughter bubbled up in his chest. Abby had surprised him. Under those soft curves of hers there was a backbone of pure steel. 'Okay. You win, it's a deal.'

'Yes…yes, a deal.' She was suddenly uncertain, lacing her fingers around her empty coffee cup. It seemed that she too needed something to occupy her when they were together. Something to take her mind off the heat that seemed to build when there was nothing practical to focus on.

'Would you like some more toast? That slice must be cold by now.'

'No. No, thanks.' She took a deep breath. 'Sorry to have spoiled your morning.'

'You didn't.' He tried to catch her eye but she seemed to be avoiding his gaze now. 'I treated you pretty badly, Abby. What you did this morning says everything about you and nothing about what I deserve.'

She seemed puzzled, but the comment emboldened her. 'I'd like you to do something else, too.'

'Go on, then. What is it?'

'I want you to call me in a couple of days, just to let me know how things are going. Will you do that?'

'Of course.' It was the least he could do. 'Or I could buy you lunch.' The words slipped out before he had a chance to stop them. But it didn't really matter. They'd be wearing snowboots in hell before she accepted. Doctors might forgive, but women didn't give you the option of standing them up a second time.

She hesitated, avoiding his gaze. 'Call me on Tuesday morning. I take my lunch at one o'clock, and if I'm free maybe we can meet up.' She picked her phone up, briskly. 'I'll make that call, then.'

CHAPTER THREE

HE'D hurt her once, and she hadn't had any say in the matter then. If he hurt her again, it was going to be her own stupid fault. But this time Abby knew the score. She wasn't at his beck and call and she wouldn't be shedding any tears over him if he decided suddenly to disappear again.

It was ten minutes' walk from the hospital to the gym they both belonged to. Abby had been taking her early-morning swims at another pool for the last six months, ever since the possibility of bumping into Nick had turned from delicious excitement to self-conscious dread. But since she hadn't let her membership lapse, for fear that might be construed as running away, she could always go for a swim if he didn't turn up.

The screens and plants in the cafeteria had been designed to break up the area and give a little privacy for each table. Abby scanned the space.

All of a sudden she didn't want to have to walk around and then be subjected to the ignominy of sitting down alone if he wasn't there.

'Hey, there.' His voice cut through her thoughts, like a hot knife through butter. 'Thanks for coming.'

She had been feeling shaky all morning, agitated at the thought of seeing Nick again, and now she was concentrating so hard on not being nervous that she'd walked straight past him. He was perched on one of the stools at the juice bar, one leg propped up on the stainless-steel rail that ran around it at low level, the other foot planted firmly on the floor.

'I said I would, didn't I?' She pulled herself up onto a stool, crossing her legs so her feet didn't dangle like a child's and putting her handbag on the empty seat she had left between Nick and herself. 'What have you got there?'

'Raspberry and apple. It's nice, want to try it?' He tilted his glass towards her.

'No, thanks. I'll have the strawberry and banana shake. And one of those toasted sandwiches, I think.' She signalled to the waitress behind the bar and gave her order, looking in her handbag for her purse. Too late. Nick had already passed a note across the bar and the waitress had taken it.

'Thanks.' Arguing with him over who was going to pay made his gesture seem more important than it was. Better to leave it. 'So how are you?'

'I'm good. I've got my appointment through.'

'Good. Dr Patel's a nice guy, and the best orthopaedic surgeon in the department. You'll be fine with him.' Jay would take care of Nick better than Abby could. Better than she had any right to.

'Thanks.' He took his change and pocketed it then felt inside his casual jacket, pulling out two foil packets and proffering them. 'And I've been keeping my side of the bargain.'

'That's okay. I'll take your word for it.' She smiled at him. 'Anyway, you could have just taken the tablets out and thrown them in the bin.'

He seemed to be considering the possibility. 'I could have. Only I would have flushed them down the sink. Always dispose of medicines safely.'

He was teasing her now and Abby felt the

coiled spring that had lodged in her stomach begin to loosen slightly. The feeling wasn't altogether agreeable. 'Well, as long as you're doing something to get the swelling down.'

He nodded. 'The ice packs are helping and the people at the pain clinic gave me some good tips. I can't put any weight on the leg still, but I can get around well enough. I might try going for a swim this afternoon.'

Unwelcome images flooded Abby's brain. Nick in the pool, water streaming across his back as he swam. Pulling himself out, the muscles of his shoulders flexing. She concentrated on his knee. 'That's not a very good idea, Nick.'

'Swimming's good exercise. The water will support my leg.'

'Dr Patel will give you some exercises and he'll be able to discuss exactly what you should and shouldn't be doing. Why don't you leave it until you see him?' She could feel her irritation level rising again. What was so important about going swimming today?

'I can't.' He dismissed her with just two words and something snapped in that part of her brain that had been filtering the anger out of her responses to him.

'Yes, you can. You just won't.' Abby jumped as a plate and glass clattered down next to her, and turned to thank the waitress, who gave her a curt nod, obviously disapproving of the sound of discord at the bar. 'Let's go and sit at one of the tables. Look, there's one free over there by the window.'

'Perfect for bullying me in private.' Nick grinned.

'I do not bully people.' If he only knew, he wouldn't say such a thing. She slid down from her stool, balanced her plate and glass in one hand, grabbed her handbag with the other and walked over to the empty table. He could follow if he liked.

As she tried to manoeuvre her way into a seat, her hands full, she saw Nick's arm reach around her, pulling the chair back so she could sink down into it. Lowering himself into the chair opposite, he smiled up at the waitress as she placed his drink in front of him. 'Thanks. That's kind of you.'

The waitress nodded and shot Abby a disapproving look. As well she might. Nick was handsome, charming and, oh, so obviously in need of a little looking after at the moment. Someone to carry his drink while he dealt with his crutches. Someone to plump his pillows and stare into his molten chocolate eyes.

'If I sound as if I don't appreciate everything you've done, Abby, that's not the case.' Nick had smiled and thanked the waitress, but now his attention was all on Abby.

'But you're just used to having things your own way.'

He grinned. 'Maybe. But I value your input.'

He made it sound as if she'd made a few suggestions, which he'd decided whether to go along with or not. Abby guessed that was about right. 'So, are you up for another piece of input?'

'Go on.'

She ignored both the smile and the dimple. Particularly the dimple. 'I think you're just falling into the same way of doing things as before. Deciding what you're going to do and then just going and doing it. I think you should wait until you can speak to your doctor and get his advice.'

'What do you think Dr Patel is going to say, then?'

'I don't second-guess colleagues. Just ask him.'

'I do have a compelling reason to get back into the water.'

Abby gave in. 'All right, so what's your compelling reason? Other than the desire to prove to yourself that you're indestructible or die trying?'

The brief tilt of his head to one side told her that she'd hit on a home truth. 'A group of us from the fire station is doing an open-water swim in five weeks' time, up in the Lake District. Actually, six of them on consecutive days. I need to be fit for that.'

The audacity of the statement made Abby choke on her drink. 'Six consecutive days? How long are these swims?'

'Between two and six miles each.'

'What? Are you completely mad, Nick? I'm all for encouraging people to exercise gently, but that's gruelling enough for anyone who's fit. It's complete and utter madness with that knee.'

He shrugged. 'I have to try. I'll see what Dr Patel says, but perhaps I can strap the leg up so that it's supported in the water.'

'No. He's going to tell you exactly what I am. You're overdoing it, and asking for trouble.' Abby couldn't believe what she was hearing.

'I thought you didn't second-guess colleagues.' His gaze was making her skin prickle.

'I don't, but I'm perfectly capable of seeing the obvious. What's so important about these swims anyway? Can't you postpone them or something? I know it's late in the year, but next spring would be much more sensible.'

He shook his head. 'It's a big charity event. There are a dozen of us swimming and we have sponsorship.'

'Well, you'll just have to drop out, then.'

He gave her an amused look. 'Are you telling me what to do?'

'I'm telling you that in my considered opinion, and I do know something about this, you'll do yourself a great deal of damage if you push yourself too hard. You'll fail with the swims and you might well put yourself into a position where you'll never get fit again. Do you want that?'

He shook his head slowly, his gaze dropping to the tabletop. 'No. But I feel I have to try. I won't push it.'

Yeah, right. Since when did Nick start anything that he didn't finish? Abby swallowed the obvious answer. Their relationship was clearly an exception to that rule. 'How much sponsorship do you have?'

'It's a hundred grand in total. I'm the only one doing all six swims and so a lot of the corporate sponsorship that we've raised depends on me. If I don't swim, we lose thirty of that.' His brow furrowed in thought. 'Maybe the sponsors will allow me to do the swims over twelve days instead of six. A day's rest in between.'

'Oh, right, that'll be okay, then. You can spend twelve days on wrecking your knee instead of six.' Concern lent a biting edge to Abby's sarcasm. She buried her face in her hands so he couldn't see her confusion. She wasn't usually this aggressive with people, but Nick was pushing all the wrong buttons with her.

His voice cut through her thoughts and she lifted her head wearily. 'It's a good cause, Abby. Maybe, when Dr Patel gives my leg the once-over, it will have improved—it already feels a lot better. I don't know right now, but surely anything is worth trying?'

The look in his eyes said it all. He knew just as well as she did that this was madness but he'd made a commitment and it was killing him not to carry it through. So he was clutching at straws. Abby sighed. 'What's the charity?'

'We're doing it in conjunction with Answers Through Sport.'

'I've heard of them. I learned to swim in one of their classes when I was a kid.'

'Really?' He was on the alert suddenly and Abby bit her lip. 'I didn't think they did general classes.'

They didn't. Abby had been a beneficiary of their *Fighting Back* programme for bullied teen-agers. But that was none of Nick's business. 'So how did you get involved with them?'

'They helped me when I was recovering from my addiction to drugs.' He shrugged. 'Now I'm returning the favour and doing some fundraising for them. They have match funding, so they'll get a grant for an amount equal to that which they raise for themselves.'

Abby's stomach twisted into a tight knot. 'So thirty grand becomes sixty.'

'Yeah. Do you see now why I won't give up without a fight? What would you do in my place?'

That was none of his business. She wasn't in his place and he had no right to ask, particularly since the answer would only encourage him in this scheme of his. 'Couldn't you get someone to step in and do the swims for you?'

'I thought of that, but we've already got everyone doing as much as they can. Even if we could find a volunteer, a month isn't long enough to build up the kind of fitness you need for something like this.' He ran his hand through his hair in a gesture of frustration. 'Why, do you know anyone?'

Abby's heart sank. Nick had no choice but to keep believing that he might just be able to do this. And now she had no choice.

'Yeah, I know someone. Me.'

* * *

Nick had refused point blank to even countenance the idea at first. But Abby had presented her credentials, competitive swimming as a teenager, member of a cross-Channel relay team when she'd been at medical school. And Nick knew as well as anyone that she was a strong enough swimmer, they'd raced together enough times at the gym.

The project committee cordially invited him to do the arithmetic. He did it and conceded. Not so cordially. But Abby had already secured the promise of two weeks' leave from work and stepped up her training.

'That's three miles.' His voice floated across the deserted swimming pool.

'No, it's not. I've got another two lengths to go. And I'd better do them quickly, before the advanced-swimmers session ends.'

He glanced at his watch. 'Yeah, the children's swimming classes will be starting in ten minutes. One final push, eh?' Nick was sitting at the side of the pool, wearing a T-shirt and sweat pants.

Tanned, relaxed and irritating beyond measure. 'Then I'll buy you breakfast.'

She didn't want him to buy her breakfast. It had taken him over a week to contact all his sponsors personally and now that was done he'd switched his attention to her. For the last two days he'd been turning up at the pool at seven o'clock in the morning to help with her training, dispensing shouted advice and encouragement that Abby doggedly ignored.

She swam another four lengths, just to show him who was boss, and found him waiting by the pool steps, one hand gripping his elbow crutch, the other holding out a large towel. 'Here you are. Don't get chilled.'

Abby wrapped the towel around herself gratefully. Being in her swimsuit when he was fully clothed, was far more uncomfortable than she had bargained for. Much more challenging than those first easy days of their acquaintance, when the guy with heart-stoppingly broad shoulders had first beaten her by two yards to the far end of the pool then smiled in her direction and exchanged a few words with her.

'Thanks.' She looked around as a group of adults and children emerged from the changing rooms. 'Looks like I won't get much more done now.'

'You've done enough.' He reached into his pocket and consulted a stopwatch. 'An hour and twenty-five. Not bad.'

'What do you mean, not bad? What's your best time?'

'One hour ten. But you did four extra lengths.'

Even if she had, she'd still have to work a little harder if she was going to match his time. But she had another three weeks to go.

'You shouldn't push yourself.' He seemed to know what she was thinking. 'An injury at this point would be bad news.'

'I know. I've done this before, remember.'

He grinned, and Abby clutched the thick towel around her tightly. 'So where do you want to go for breakfast? As it's Saturday, we can take our time.'

Breakfast in the presence of Nick's smile sounded fantastic, but it was forbidden fruit. On the other hand, she needed to eat and at this rate she'd be gnawing her own arm off before she managed to get rid of him. 'What about that place across the road? They do fresh croissants and a latte to die for.'

'Sure. Whatever you want. I'll meet you in the lobby...' Nick seemed to realise that he'd lost Abby's attention and that it was now fixed on a small group of children on the other side of the pool.

It was nothing. Just high jinks, kids mucking about. Abby kept her eye on the group anyway.

'So I'll meet you in the lobby in ten minutes?'

'Yeah, ten minutes...' The shrill voices of the children swelled above the mounting noise in the pool and Abby strained to see what was going on.

'What is it?' She could feel his fingers brushing her elbow lightly, and she jerked her arm away. She had neither the time nor the inclination to stop and discuss this with Nick. Abby marched round to the other side of the pool and approached the group of children.

There was a little girl at the centre, red in the face and obviously trying to hold back tears, as one of the older girls made jokes that everyone else seemed to think were funny. She'd been that child. Surrounded by a ring of distorted faces, trying not to cry at their taunts. Hoping that someone would come along and break it up. And now Abby had the chance to do something that no one had ever bothered to do for her. She had to get this right.

'Excuse me.' Abby had to shoulder her way through the group to reach the child. 'I just wanted to ask you where you got your swimming costume? I'm looking for one for my niece, and this is so pretty.'

As she spoke, the group melted away, re-forming a few yards away behind Abby's back. She ignored them and knelt down next to the little girl, leaning in to hear her whispered reply.

'Really? I was in there the other day and I didn't see any pink ones.' Abby smiled encouragingly. 'I'll have to go back and take another look.'

She got a hesitant smile back, which felt like pure gold, and the sick feeling in her stomach began to subside a little. The child reached forward and pulled at Abby's towel. 'Does yours have flowers?'

'No, worse luck.' Abby unwrapped the towel, wrinkling her nose. 'Just plain blue. Not as pretty as yours.'

Another smile. This time bright and clear, the way a child should smile. 'Which swimming class are you in, sweetie?'

'Over there.' Abby followed the little girl's pointing finger to a group of younger children at the shallow end of the pool, supervised by two women.

'Well, why don't you go and join them? But there's something I'd like to tell you first.'

'Okay.' Half the child's attention was already on her playmates.

'If anyone ever hurts you or makes fun of you, you should tell an adult. Your mum or dad, or one of your teachers.' That hadn't worked too well for Abby, but it didn't mean it wasn't good advice in general. 'Will you remember that?'

'All right.' The child nodded solemnly and scuttled away, the jibes of the older girls seemingly forgotten. Abby sat back on her heels and took a deep breath to steady herself. The adult in her told her that banging the bullies' heads together and throwing them in the pool wasn't going to help anyone, least of all their victim. The child in her was itching to do just that.

The sound of feet scuffling on the tiles as the group behind her broke up, saved her from herself. Abby turned and saw Nick approaching and got to her feet, pulling the towel back around her.

'You're shivering.' He'd followed her to the bench at the side of the pool and lowered himself down next to her.

She wasn't shivering, she was trembling. There was a difference and Nick knew it as well as she did. 'I'm okay. I should let someone know…'

'Go and get dressed.' He indicated the children's swimming coach with a nod of his head. 'I'll let Diane know what's happened.'

He was right. She had to let go of this, pass it over to the people who were best placed to do something. It was hard, though. Abby had worked through the fear and self-loathing from her own childhood but seeing another child bullied had created a whole new set of emotions. Anger and helplessness had smacked her hard in the face, leaving her reeling.

'Go and get changed.' He had already caught Diane's eye and was pulling himself to his feet, grabbing his crutches.

There was nothing for it but to do as he said. Abby sat for a moment, watching Nick and Diane as they talked. It was okay. Everything was going to be okay. She repeated the words over to herself as she made her way towards the entrance to the changing rooms.

Nick only had to get out of his sweatpants and canvas shoes then pull on a pair of jeans, but when he made it to the reception area he found that Abby was already there, waiting for him. 'Is she all right?' She fired the words at him almost before he had reached her.

'She's fine. Diane's talked to her and she's going to have a word with the mother. She asked me to thank you for spotting what was going on and breaking it up.'

She nodded wordlessly, her eyes fixed on the floor. It seemed that what he'd done met with her approval.

'You ready for breakfast, then?' Maybe he'd ask her. About that haunted look in her eyes and the way she'd reacted at the poolside. The way she was reacting now.

'I'm a little tired. Maybe another time.'

He supposed that 'another time' meant when he'd forgotten all about what had happened here this morning. That wasn't going to happen. 'Abby, I know that no case of bullying should be taken lightly...' he didn't know quite how to put this '...but you seem very upset.'

The look in her eyes told him that he was right. She'd chosen to see something else, something that she remembered rather than what had actually gone on here. But her lips, pressed together tightly, showed that she wasn't about to admit anything of the sort. 'I'm tired, Nick, and I didn't react appropriately. It was a mistake.'

'Our mistakes often tell us more than anything.' Nick smiled to soften the words. It wasn't a criticism. Or if it was, it was aimed primarily at himself.

'And what this one tells me is that I'm tired and I need to get home.'

'Are you sure?' He shouldn't be questioning her like this. Or rather he shouldn't care so much.

If he didn't care about her answers, then asking would have been okay.

He was about to get the brush-off—he could almost see the lie forming on her lips. He caught her gaze, searching her pale blue eyes, and for a moment he saw the truth and wanted to hold Abby, protect her from every real and imagined threat.

'I'm going home, Nick.' She swung her swimming bag onto her shoulder and would have walked away from him if he'd let her.

He'd cared too much, pushed her too hard, and now she'd drawn back. Nick preferred not to think about what that mistake said about him. 'I'll drop by later in the week with the detailed itinerary.'

'Good. Thanks.'

'Keep up the good work.'

'Right.' There was no stopping her from going, this time. She turned and walked away from him, turning in the doorway to give him a wave that looked far more like *Goodbye and good riddance* than *See you later*, and then she was gone.

CHAPTER FOUR

EUSTON station was crowded, rush-hour commuters streaming from trains and making their way in a concentrated mass to the Underground escalators. Abby stood in the most open spot she could, studying the departure boards. The train for Windermere was an estimated twelve minutes late, which meant there was over half an hour to wait.

No one was here yet. No Nick at the platform entrance, where they'd said they'd meet, and the swarms of people on the station concourse were making her head swim.

Standing on her toes, Abby could see a coffee shop in one corner of the station. There was a queue of people waiting for their early morning shot, but at least she'd have somewhere to stand where her case wasn't constantly being bumped by passers-by.

She fixed her eyes on her destination and began to march determinedly towards it. She hated crowds. Rush-hour commuting was an art, and she'd got used to it, but she'd never managed to completely lose the feeling of unease at being confronted with a faceless, potentially antagonistic mass of people. And her nerves at the thought of seeing Nick again, despite the fact that they'd been in almost daily contact by email, weren't helping particularly.

There was a wait for the coffee, but as soon as she had the warm cardboard beaker in her hand she began to feel better. Now all she had to do was find a quiet corner to drink it in. She waited while another stream of people walked briskly past. Her stomach was still churning and she needed to sit down, sip her drink and get herself together.

'Oh!' Someone had collided with her case, kicked it to one side and kept walking. The plastic top flew off the beaker of coffee as Abby's fingers tightened instinctively around it, and hot liquid spilled onto her fleece jacket and dribbled onto the floor.

Nothing like looking where you're going! The words shot through her head, but she was suddenly too breathless to mutter them after the man. Her hands were full, coffee in one hand, case in the other, the straps of her handbag beginning to slip from her shoulder. As another wave of anonymous faces headed straight for her, Abby scurried towards the only form of cover she could reach, an information board at the edge of the concourse, and leaned against it for support.

'Not now. *Not now!*' She muttered the instruction to herself under her breath, so softly that even she couldn't hear the words. Her lungs were straining for air and her heart thumped in her chest as if it had decided that it wanted out and the most direct route was straight through her ribcage.

'Breathe. One…two…' Her words were louder and touched with desperation this time, but that didn't seem to make much difference. She was gulping in air too fast and a feeling of nameless, shapeless dread was beginning to engulf her.

'Everything's okay. Just slow down.' Abby tried again to convince her own body to respond, closing her eyes in concentration and then snapping them back open again as the world swam and she almost toppled over.

'Abby?' Someone was there. Someone who smelled like Nick. Soft leather and sandalwood, gasped into her heaving lungs and then breathed out again far too quickly.

'Give her some space.' His voice rang out. Commanding enough to divert the flow of people away from them. An arm around her shoulders pulled her into the protection of his body and she clung to him, letting him prise the half-empty beaker of coffee from the convulsive grip of her fingers.

'Slowly, Abby. Breathe slowly. On my count… One…two…three.'

For a moment, her heaving lungs listened and complied with his instructions, where they had ignored her own. But then the noise in her ears and the banging of her heart, craving more oxygen than was strictly good for it, took over again. She was dimly aware of someone stopping, and that Nick had spoken to them, but right now all she could think of was that she had to get out of there.

'Okay, Abby. Everything's okay. Come with me.' He tried to move her, and she clutched instinctively for the handle of her case. 'It's all right. Someone's bringing your bag. We're just going outside to sit down.'

Sit down. Yes. She'd like to sit down. She'd be okay in a minute if she could just sit down. She felt the slightly uneven sway of Nick's body against hers as he led her through the automatic doors and out into the fresh air.

'Would you mind? Thank you. No, she just needs to sit for a moment. Thanks.' Nick had cleared a space for her on a nearby bench and Abby sank down onto it gratefully. Someone moved up and he sat down next to her, his arm around her shoulder.

Her chest was still heaving frantically. 'Anyone got a paper bag? Yeah, large one.' His voice again. 'Thanks.' Nick shook the bag out and put it into her trembling fingers. 'You know what to do, Abby. That's right.'

He helped her put the bag up to her lips and she

took a breath. Then another. And another. That was better. There were a few crumbs left on the inside of the bag and she smelled the rich smell of almond paste. Must be the remains of an almond croissant.

'Better?' Nick was holding her, not tightly but close enough to let her know that he was there. That someone was there.

'Yes…thanks. Sorry.'

'Don't you worry about it.' A smartly dressed woman was bending down in front of her, and she brushed Abby's knee with well-manicured fingers. 'I get panic attacks, too. You'll be okay in a minute.'

A single tear of mortification prickled at the side of Abby's eye and she brushed it away before Nick got a chance to see it. 'Sorry to make such a fuss.'

'Hey, there. You don't need to apologise.' Nick gently slipped the straps of her handbag from her shoulder, and she realised that she had been hugging it tightly to her side. 'Let go. That's right.'

'She's all wet.' The manicured fingers brushed at her fleece, ineffectually.

'Yeah, let's get this off you, Abby.' Nick pulled at the zipper and had her out of it in a second. Obviously the result of practice. 'Your T-shirt doesn't look too bad. Just a few drops.'

She drew her arms across her body, shivering despite the warmth of the morning breeze. Nick wrapped his jacket around her shoulders and she snuggled into it, wondering if she could some-how contrive to disappear.

At least he took the task off her shoulders of thanking the concerned passers-by and sending them on their way. Finally they were alone, his arm still protectively draped across the back of the bench behind her.

'We'd better get going. We'll miss our train.' Abby made an attempt at a smile.

'We've already missed it.'

'What?' Surely it hadn't been a whole half-hour since she looked at the passenger informa-tion board. Had she blacked out or something?

'You're not getting on that train, and neither am I. I want to know what's bothering you.'

'Nothing. It's nothing, Nick.'

'In that case, you're not getting on any train.'

He sat quite still, waiting for her to call his bluff. If it was a bluff. Abby doubted it somehow.

She took a breath. The feeling of dread that still clung to her receded slightly and a small, treacherous voice at the back of her head taunted her. Nick had seen her weakness now. She was vulnerable.

'What do you mean, not getting on any train?'

'Someone who gets panic attacks when nothing's wrong shouldn't be swimming in open water.' His lips quirked slightly. 'You're a health and safety hazard, Abby.'

'I'm not!'

'Then something's wrong and you're going to tell me about it.' She opened her mouth to protest and he held one finger up. 'Not here. There's a little coffee shop around the corner. You'll have a hot drink and something to eat and then you'll tell me. I'm guessing you skipped breakfast this morning.'

Abby deprived him of the satisfaction of being right by not answering. Unzipping her case, she slid a clean sweater out and pulled it over her head. Nick put his jacket back on with the hint of a grin, almost as if he was savouring the fact that she'd left a little of her scent on it, and Abby wondered whether punching him would seem ungrateful.

He was, at least, trying to put her at her ease. Avoiding the crowds. Letting her walk close to him and soak up the comfort of his bulk alongside her. Making her laugh despite herself. But Abby knew that there was no way of getting out of his questions. He was just waiting for the right time and, when it came, no amount of silence on her part was going to do for an answer.

'Feeling better now?' He'd watched while she'd downed a tall, creamy latte and a blueberry muffin, sipping his herbal tea thoughtfully.

'Yes. Thanks.' Here it came.

'So, I have this problem. There's no way in the world that I'm going to let you get on that train if the trip is stressing you out so badly that it's giving you panic attacks. Can you help me with that?'

His gaze held her fast, trapped in the most tender of bonds, and Abby gave up the struggle. 'It's nothing to do with the swimming, Nick, I'm fine with that, really. I used to get panic attacks a lot when I was a teenager. I grew out of them.'

'Plainly. That's why you were breathing into a paper bag just now.'

'I was watching the time, trying to find the right platform, and I spilled my coffee and…there were just too many people all of a sudden.'

'I guess crowds can be pretty intimidating at times. Particularly for someone who's been bullied.' He'd obviously been thinking about this, put two and two together and come up with four.

'Yeah. I guess they probably can.'

'And that was when you learned to swim? Why you went to the charity for help?'

'You don't miss much, do you?'

He shrugged. 'Not when it comes to you, Abby.'

'I don't know what you mean.'

His dark eyes registered the lie and immediately forgave it. 'Did the swimming help?'

'Yes, it helped. It wasn't just the swimming, they held counselling sessions as well. I got to meet other kids, some of them suffering much more than I did, and I didn't feel so alone with it.'

'What about your parents?' He was unerring in picking up what should have been there but hadn't been. The things she purposely hadn't said.

She shrugged, trying to make out it was nothing. 'They played bridge with one of the ringleader's parents. Didn't want to make waves, so they pretended it wasn't happening.'

'So you did it all on your own.'

'Yeah.' All of it. She'd beaten the bullies. Won a place at medical school. Worked hard to get the letters after her name and the title of Doctor before it. 'The people at Answers Through Sport taught me how to be proud of myself. Of what I achieved.'

Abby planted her hands on the table, palms down, in a signal that this particular show-and-tell session was at an end. 'It was a long time ago, Nick. I've left that all behind me. We all have our bad days.'

He nodded an acknowledgement. 'As long as that's all it is. You talked me out of swimming because it wasn't worth sacrificing my health.

I'm more than happy to return the favour if it's causing you any problems.'

'What, and lose thirty thousand pounds? Sixty, if you count the match funding.'

'That's exactly what I said to you, and look how far it got me.' He grinned. 'I can find another way of raising the money. Maybe I'll make you run for it instead.'

'I hate running. And my swimming's an answer to whatever problems I might have, not the cause. I'm looking forward to the swim and you know I can do it.'

'Of course you can. Better than I could, even without having injured my knee.'

'Now, there's an admission.' Abby managed a smile without having to force herself.

'Well, you caught me in a moment of weakness.' He grinned back at her. 'So, what is it? Whatever you want to do now is okay.'

'That thirty grand is ours, Nick. You raised the sponsorship and I'm going to collect it. And then Answers Through Sport is going to collect another thirty thousand on the back of it.'

He chuckled. 'Sounds good to me. We'll all have one hell of a party when we're done, I promise.'

They made the next train with ten minutes to spare. Abby slid into the seat opposite Nick's, waiting for him to settle himself comfortably, his leg stretched out under the small table that separated them, before she carefully tucked her feet under her own seat, not letting them touch his.

The next three hours promised to be long ones. She tried to concentrate on her book while Nick immersed himself in something on his laptop. Rubbing his temple in thought. A slow smile, when he caught her looking at him. It was like watching a commercial for men's cologne. Distracting.

Finally, she gave up and laid her book down. 'What's that you're doing? More arrangements for the swim?'

He grinned. 'No—I think that's all done.'

'That's a relief. I was wondering if you were about to email me again with another set of instructions for something.'

'No, nothing like that. Are you saying that my emails were unappreciated?'

'No. Just that you're very thorough.' Actually, Nick's emails had been great. Brief, to the point, and covering everything she needed to know about the arrangements for the swim. And she'd looked for them over the last few weeks, disappointed when they hadn't come, and there was no excuse for her to type a short reply.

'Well, this is nothing to do with swimming. It's some work I'm doing with the fire brigade up in Cumbria.' He paused. The slight curl of his lips told Abby that he was waiting for her to ask.

'In Cumbria? That's very convenient. Since we're actually on our way there now.'

'That's what I thought.' One eyelid flickered and then he grinned. 'The guy I'm working with is my old station commander, Ted Bishop. He was promoted and came up to Cumbria a couple of years back. The idea for the swim came up when a few of us went up to visit him last year. He's been very helpful with the fun day, helping us to get a good location and all the necessary permits.'

'So this isn't just an excuse to overdo it when you're supposed to be on light duties, is it?'

'No!' He flashed her a smile. 'Anyway, there's

no strain on my knee involved, I'm acting as a consultant. Ted knows that I've done some work on arson and he approached me directly. There's been a spate of attacks in the area he's responsible for, and we need to catch whoever's doing it before anyone gets hurt. Seems I may have something to add to the equation.'

Nick always had something to add to any equation. 'You mean forensics?'

He chuckled, relaxing back into his seat. 'Nothing that fashionable, I'm afraid. After I joined the fire service I did some courses in my spare time and ended up doing an MA in psychology. That led me to some work in conjunction with the university on the motivations and behaviour of fire-raisers. I've been helping Ted with some profiling.'

'Sounds interesting.' Abby was almost holding her breath. The whole time she'd known Nick he had never willingly offered any information about his past, and even these morsels were fascinating beyond their own limited worth. 'You studied psychology before you became a fire-fighter?'

'No. I originally studied to be a structural engineer. I volunteered for the Fire and Emergency Support Services when I was at university and after I graduated I decided to change direction.'

'And you've never looked back?'

There was something free, clear and unbearably intimate about his short chuckle. This was more than just the idle exchange of information on a long train journey. She was finally getting to know Nick, understand some of the things that made him tick. They'd skipped that part last time, and Abby was beginning to wish they hadn't. If she'd known then what she knew now, it might have saved her a whole world of grief.

'Never. Not for a moment as far as my decision to join the fire service is concerned. Anyway, looking back is… Sometimes it's not helpful.' He caught her eye and she was lost for a moment in his gaze. Dragged across the line that she'd drawn between them, which said that anything unconnected with the swim was a no-go area. Abby shifted slightly in her seat, aware that her right leg was getting pins and needles.

She reached down to rub it, thankful for the distraction.

'You okay there? I'm taking up all the space.' Nick didn't wait for an answer but reached down under the table, grasping her ankle and propping it up against his leg. 'Is that better?'

This was more than just getting comfortable on a long train journey. He'd tried to apologise to her, more than once, and Abby hadn't let him. She itemised the layers between her skin and his. His thick denim jeans. Her lighter ones. Her sock. Her trainer. There were many miles in front of them and this one, small acknowledgement that maybe they could forget the past and start again didn't seem so much to ask.

'Yes. Thanks.'

'Stretch out a bit.'

Abby stretched her cramped legs and changed the subject. 'So you'll be away working with the fire service in Cumbria while we're up there?'

'No. I'm just finishing up now. When we get to Windermere I'll be officially on holiday.'

'Unless anything else comes up.' Abby doubted

that Nick would split hairs about being on leave if he was needed.

'Yeah. But I'd prefer not to admit to that, if you don't mind. Ted's already promised to call me if he needs me.' He looked up as the refreshments trolley rattled up the confined space of the aisle. 'Would you like anything?'

'No. Thanks. I might close my eyes for a little while.' Abby was tired now. This always seemed to happen after a panic attack. As soon as it was over and she was somewhere that she felt safe, she'd feel unbearably weary.

'Yeah. Try and relax. It's already been a full morning.' He grinned at her and Abby closed her eyes. Soon enough, pretending to sleep gave way to real sleep.

Sam and the rest of the group were already there when they arrived at the hotel, and Abby found herself engulfed in a group of friendly, easygoing firefighters. With a dozen other people to claim his attention, Nick's overwhelming presence seemed to dilute a little, and she began to relax. The group migrated from the lounge to the dining area then back again to the lounge, and she left them swapping stories and laughing together and made her way up to bed early.

Even if she'd woken with a start, early and in an unfamiliar bed, she'd slept well. The bright, crisp morning that awaited her when she drew back the curtains had all the promise of a warm, sunny day, and Abby showered and dressed, ready to face the morning. Today was a day to take things easy, before the swimming started tomorrow.

Drawn outside by sunshine and the promise of the lake, she wandered along a well-worn track from the hotel to the waterside. Lake Windermere, the largest of the Cumbrian lakes, was silent in the early morning. Waterbirds plunged their heads beneath the shimmering surface, diving for their food. A small boat moved across the water, going about its business against a backdrop of stunning beauty.

'Nice day.' Nick's voice interrupted her thoughts as she sat staring across the lake. This time it was the real thing and not an echo from her dreams. 'How did you sleep?'

'Well, thanks. I think it's the air up here.' Abby

turned and saw Nick behind her, leaning on a walking stick. 'Hey, where's your crutch gone?'

He grinned. 'I haven't thrown it away quite yet, it's up in my room. But I've graduated onto this.' He sat down next to her on the grass. 'So, how are you feeling about the swim tomorrow?'

'Two miles. Piece of cake. Look how calm the water is.'

'Yeah. Hope it stays this way. The weather forecast's good.'

'Stop fretting. We'll do the swim in the morning, and then there's the fun day in the afternoon. I hope it's going to be good.'

'It'll be great.' He flopped back on the grass, squinting up at the sky. 'There's a couple of bands, sideshows, refreshments tent. Organised sports for the kids…'

'Bouncy castle?'

'Wouldn't be without one. Why, do you fancy trying it out? Climb right to the top and let down your golden hair.' He reached forward and tugged at the plait, which reached halfway down Abby's back.

'Not long enough.'

'Hmm. I'll bring a ladder.'

'Oh, and how are you going to get up it with that knee?'

'I'm a firefighter. We're good with ladders. It's all part of the job.'

'You miss it, don't you?' Abby leaned back on one elbow. She'd seen the way Nick's eyes had gleamed when the talk last night had turned to work.

'Yep.' His heavy lids dropped over his eyes for a moment in a brief expression of regret. 'I wish it hadn't ended this way.'

'Ended? But I thought Dr Patel had already signed you off for light duties. There's no reason you can't go back to active duty in a few months.' Abby bit her lip. She'd hoped that Nick wouldn't find out that she had been checking with Jay Patel on his progress.

'That's right. Apparently I'm a far better patient than he thought I might be.' A grin hovered around his lips. 'Probably because one of his colleagues softened me up a bit first. I'm not going back to active duty, though.'

'Is that…your decision?' Why would Nick

throw a job that he loved away when he didn't need to?

'Yes. I have a new job, a promotion. Disaster planning, fire prevention. I get to run my own unit. I applied before my injury and I heard a few weeks ago that I'd got it.'

'So…that's good, isn't it?' Nick was studying the clear blue sky, and Abby couldn't make out what he was thinking.

'Yeah. Yes, it is. It's a great opportunity to make a real difference. I'll be involved with the public, with fire crews in my area. It's what I want.'

'But not so much ever since it looked like you might not have a choice? Since your injury turned everything upside down?' Abby rolled over onto her stomach, next to him.

He grinned at her. 'Yeah.'

'So what *did* you want when you applied for the job? When you did have the choice?'

Nick chuckled. 'Okay. Allow me a little irrational regret, will you?'

'As long as you know it *is* irrational.'

'I do now.' His eyes were dark in the sunlight. Tender and unbearably unsettling.

A wedge of geese flew overhead, and Abby craned her neck, following their path out across the water. 'Isn't it time for breakfast? I'm starving.' She got to her feet.

'Not yet. They don't start serving breakfast for another half-hour.' He levered himself upwards, grabbing his stick. 'Why don't we take a walk, down by the edge of the lake?'

The cool, blue water beckoned her. 'Yes, that would be nice.'

They scrambled down the steep incline that led down to the water's edge and gained a narrow path which ran beside the lake. Walking side by side meant that they had to move closer, and when Nick offered his arm Abby did what had previously been unthinkable and took it. As soon as she was connected to his warmth, allowing it to filter into her bones, it didn't seem such a bad idea and she allowed her hand to stay curled around the crook of his elbow.

'This is a nice spot. The hotel's lovely. And this

part of the lake is really quiet.' Abby turned her face up, towards the sun.

'Yeah. We chose somewhere away from the main tourist area so that we'd have a place to rest and recharge our batteries.'

'Good idea. I feel as if I've just dropped off the edge of the world for a while, it's so peaceful.'

'No more panic attacks, then?' The tension in his tone told Abby that this was the question he'd been working his way around to. Maybe even sought her out to ask.

'No. I feel as if I could take the world on today.'

'And win?'

'Of course.'

'Single-handedly, no doubt.'

'What other way is there?'

He seemed to find something funny in that. Abby fixed him with a warning stare and he shrugged. 'So we should enjoy today, then?'

'Yeah. Tomorrow will come soon enough.'

Nick didn't reply. His eyes were fixed on the cloudless sky, as if he were pondering some basic truth of the universe and the answer was up there somewhere.

He stopped suddenly. His stick fell to the ground, but Abby hardly noticed that because Nick was holding her. His heat. His scent. The bulk of his body. Protective and dangerous, all at the same time.

'Nick…what…what are you doing?'

'Wondering if you'd like some company. We could enjoy today together.' He brushed his lips against hers, his eyes half beckoning, half mesmerising. Slowly, almost as if it was beyond her control to stop it, she felt her hand move up to his cheek, saw her fingers caress the side of his face.

'Since we're on holiday…' We can do as we please. He didn't say it, but she knew that was what he meant. And what couldn't she do with Nick? His lips. His body.

Abby couldn't think. Only that she wanted him to do it. Kiss her and be done with it. It couldn't possibly be any more erotic than her imaginings. Only she'd imagined him holding her, too, and the reality of his embrace was far better. Tentatively she ran her fingers across his lips and felt them form into the shape of a kiss.

She hadn't expected anything polite or restrained from Nick. He was a man who took what he wanted, and when he kissed her he took everything and didn't stop until her head was spinning and her body was moulding itself to his of its own accord. He challenged her, invading her senses with raw passion that had a golden thread of tenderness in its weave.

When he drew back, she knew that it was only because he wanted more from her. Winding her fingers through his hair, she pulled his head down, towards hers again. For a moment he resisted, just to show her that he could, and then a teasing smile curved his lips and he gave way. Kissed her again. And again.

'Abby…' That one, broken word told her everything. His soul-crushing rejection of her hadn't been because he didn't want her. It had been something else.

'Why, Nick? What's changed in the last six months?'

'I'm not the man who can give you what you deserve, not long term. But you said it yourself that this is like taking time out of our lives. What happens here can stay here.'

She couldn't believe she was even thinking about it. Nick had already hurt her once and even though she'd forgiven him for that now, she'd not rescinded the promise she'd made to herself that he wouldn't get the opportunity to do so again. But she knew the score now. Abby understood Nick a great deal better than she had the last time, and knew he wasn't in this for keeps. She could take what she'd been craving for so many months now and then go home, before he had a chance to break her heart.

He drew back, and the breeze from the water suddenly made her shiver. Each of her senses were acute and vulnerable, as if they'd been woken from a long sleep. She wanted more. And he deliberately gave her nothing.

'Think about it.'

It was all she could think about, but that didn't stop her from still being afraid. Afraid of reaching out and finding he wasn't there. Or that he was. Abby didn't know which terrified her most. 'I'm not sure, Nick.'

He kissed her again, just a whisper on her lips but all her senses exploded. She knew now what else he could do. From now on, even his most casual touch wouldn't be the same. His dark, velvet eyes held unthinkable secrets that offered themselves to her.

'Good. Means you *are* thinking about it.'

CHAPTER FIVE

NICK didn't seem to expect an answer straight away—in fact, he seemed intent on not having one, obviously content to let her simmer for a while. He'd made his bid for her, and now he was waiting for her to respond. That was fine. If she couldn't resist him, at least she could keep him waiting, not fall straight into his arms like the awkward, stupid girl she felt herself to be.

Opening the door to the lobby of the hotel, he ushered her inside.

'Here they are.' Mrs Pearce, the proprietor, was sitting behind the reception desk, and she nodded her too-bright, bronzed curls towards a young man.

'There's someone here to see you, hen.'

Nick accepted the endearment with a smiling nod and advanced towards the young man, his right hand held out. 'Hi. Nick Hunter.'

'Graham Edson. I'm with the local paper. Nice to meet you.' Graham looked Nick over quickly. 'You're doing the swim with that?' He pointed at Nick's walking stick.

'No, my injury made me drop out.' He was standing between Abby and Graham, and his broad bulk almost completely shielded the smaller man from Abby's view. 'A friend is swimming for me.'

Just *a friend*. No hesitation. All the way back to the hotel she'd been wondering if she might not mean a little more to Nick than that, and now he'd put her firmly back in her place. 'That'll be me.' Abby skirted around Nick and nodded at Graham. 'Abby Maitland.'

'Oh. Nice to meet you.' Graham's attention was all on her now. 'Are you a fireman, too? Fire-woman, I mean. Fireperson...'

Abby saw Nick's eyes roll behind Graham's back. Louise, the newest member of Nick's crew, had been joking last night about how no one ever knew what to call her. 'It's firefighter. And, no, I'm not, I'm a doctor.'

'Ah. And you've stepped in to try and cover the

swim.' Graham was looking her up and down, and the small hairs at the back of Abby's neck bristled. He was affable, unremarkable and Abby didn't much like his assumptions. Just trying wasn't an option.

'I'll be doing all six of the courses in Nick's place.'

'Hmm. I'd like to get some details about you for my paper, if that's all right. I'm doing an article.'

'Sure...' Abby reckoned that any publicity was good publicity.

'Our organiser has a press pack, giving details of the events and biographies of all the swimmers,' Nick broke in. 'If you'll give me your email address, I'll get one sent through to you this morning.'

He reached into his jacket, pulling out a notebook, and as he did so his keys jangled to the floor. Quick as a flash, Graham had pounced on them, holding them for a moment in his hand before he gave them back to Nick.

'Unusual key fob.'

Abby's stomach tightened, but Nick didn't waver. 'Yeah. What's your email address?'

Graham's eyes were on him as he reeled off the address and Nick took it down. Then he turned his attention back onto Abby. 'I just wanted to ask a few extra questions.' The journalist motioned her to one of the seats behind him and sat down next to her. 'As a doctor, I assume you're aware of the health risks of open-water swimming.'

He'd pulled a small voice recorder out of his jacket pocket and was aiming it at Abby. Fine. She could handle this.

'If you want to know our policy on health and safety, you should speak to the team's official medical spokesman.' Nick was there again. He seemed determined not to let Abby get a single word out.

'Yes, but personally...' Graham leaned closer and ignored Nick '...you must have thought about this? Weil's disease, for instance. Are you happy to take those risks?'

Nick reached around her, switching off the recorder in Graham's hand. The look on his face told Abby that he was exercising some restraint, not ripping the gizmo from the reporter's grasp and stamping on it. 'You'll have to forgive us, but we're busy right now. As I said, Pete Welsh, who is the events organiser, will email you the press pack this morning and he's available here to answer all your questions. Much better than we can, I imagine.'

He could speak for himself on that one. But the pressure of his fingers on her shoulder silenced Abby. She supposed it was better to leave it until she had Nick alone before she voiced her objections.

'Okay, fine.' Graham rose and pulled a card from his pocket, handing it to Abby. 'I've already got the press pack so I won't keep you if you're busy. I'd like to speak with you later, though.'

'I'll be here.' Abby took the card he proffered and put it into her pocket. Nick may think that kissing her gave him the right to decide who she could and couldn't speak to but he was wrong on that score. Dead wrong.

She waited while Nick walked to the main doors with Graham, virtually escorting him off the premises, and watched as the man got into his car and drove away. 'What was that all about?'

'I didn't like his questions.'

'That's obvious.' Abby blocked his path as he went to walk back into the lobby. 'I am capable of answering questions about health risks, you know. I do it every day.'

'This is different.'

'Different how? Nick, please tell me that you're not worried I'll get it wrong. I may specialise in orthopaedics but I haven't quite forgotten my general training yet.'

He stared at her, and Abby stood her ground. She wasn't moving until he gave her an answer. 'No. I don't think that. But your position, as a doctor, gives more weight to what you say.'

'So I know what I'm talking about. Doesn't that make my opinion more valid?'

'Yes, it does, that's my whole point. It's not the official one, though. You know as well as I do that, although the risk of catching Weil's disease is pretty much negligible, it can't be ruled out entirely.'

Abby threw up her hands in frustration. 'It's an acceptable level of risk. Made even less by the fact that we're wearing wetsuits, so there's no chance of infected water getting into any cuts or abrasions.'

'Right. An acceptable level of risk. Which means it's not an impossibility.' Nick let out an exasperated breath. 'What happens if you get quoted out of context, or your words get twisted to give the impression that precautions don't need to be taken with open-water swimming? If some-one acted on that, it would leave you to answer for the consequences.'

'I guess that would depend on the circum-stances. I'm not sure.' She was beginning to catch his meaning.

'Exactly. The press pack covers all that and it's worded very carefully. This guy's already got a copy of it and yet he wants an off-the-cuff medi-cal opinion on a complex issue in a hotel lobby. Doesn't that tell you something?'

Now she thought about it, it did. Nick had been looking out for her. Unwilling to back down, and unable to honestly tell him that he was wrong, Abby simply stared at him.

'What are you two bickering about so early in the morning?' Pete's voice sounded by the stairs and both Nick and Abby swung round to face the retired firefighter.

'We are not...'

'Bickering.' Abby reddened as she heard Nick echo her words.

Pete chuckled. 'Well, there's something you both agree on.' He was making for the dining room and his step hardly faltered. 'Don't miss breakfast. We've got plenty to do today if we're going to be ready for Windermere tomorrow.'

Day One. Two miles. Lake Windermere.

'How did you do that?' Louise was grinning at Abby.

'What?'

'I saw you five minutes ago and you weren't wearing your wetsuit. It takes me half an hour to get into mine.'

'Didn't anyone show you the shopping-bag trick?' Abby liked Louise. She was the youngest of the firefighters in the group, but she gave no quarter and expected none back. Didn't trade on the fact that she was a woman, and the others obviously respected her for it.

'No. Go on, then. Show me the secret formula.'

'Here, put your foot into this plastic bag… Right, then slip your foot into the wetsuit, like so.' Abby helped Louise draw the neoprene up her right leg then pulled the bag off her foot. 'See, the wetsuit doesn't cling to your foot when you put it on. Do that with the other foot and your hands and it's easy.'

Louise wriggled into her wetsuit, and Abby zipped the back up for her. 'Yeah, that's good. Thanks.'

'Swing your arms around, make sure you've got plenty of movement at the shoulders.' Abby nodded in satisfaction. 'Yes, that's right.'

'Nick says that you've swum the Channel.' Louise was staring out over the water.

'As part of a relay team. I didn't swim the whole way.' Louise was obviously nervous and wanted some reassurance. 'Listen, you've done your training.'

'Yes. Nick's been checking up on us all. I thought he'd get off our backs a bit when he came back to work, but he's even worse now. Being on limited duties is driving him mad.'

'I imagine it would be.' Abby grinned. 'But you've swum in open water before.'

'Yep. It was part of our training schedule, we all went away for the weekend...' Louise broke off. The confident young woman that Abby had met less than two days ago was gnawing at her lower lip. 'I just don't want to let anyone down.'

'You won't.' Abby hesitated for a moment. It would have been nice to have completed this swim ahead of everyone else, if only to show Nick that she could, and she let go of the idea with a stab of regret. 'Tell you what. Why don't you swim with me? We'll do this one together.'

Louise shrugged. 'I can't keep up. The guys are much stronger swimmers than I am and, from what Nick says, so are you.'

'Then I'll slow down a bit. What do you say?'

'I think if both the women come last, we'll be in for a ribbing. I reckoned that you might be the one to keep our end up.'

'Forget that.' Abby wondered if this really was her talking. The competitive spirit who didn't let anything stand in her way once she was in the water because being the butt of that kind of joke was for losers. Maybe she'd mellowed with age. 'Listen, if they think this is all about winning, they're wrong. It's all about helping each other to complete the course and raise the money we need. That's why you decided to do it, wasn't it?'

Louise brightened. 'Yes. One of the guys at the station has a daughter who's a wheelchair user and he and his wife have to travel miles to get her to a therapy pool. I really wanted to help, but I'm not sure now that I haven't bitten off more than I can chew.'

'Like I said, you've done the training. From what I know about Nick, he wouldn't let you swim if he didn't think you could do it.'

'Right in one.' Nick's voice boomed out behind her. 'You know how to do this, Lou. Work as a team, rely on your training. And follow whatever advice you hear me shout in your direction.'

'Advice!' Louise's eyebrows shot up and Abby suppressed a chuckle. Since when did Nick give advice?

'It's orders at work. Advice here. Only I will be watching you, every step of the way, to make sure you take it.' He was good at this. His easy manner and solid dependability inspired confidence and Abby could see why all his crew held him in such high regard. 'Why don't you go and warm up now? It's about time.'

'Suppose so.' Louise gave Abby a shy smile. 'I'd like to swim with you, if that's okay.'

'Good. I'd like that too.' Abby went to follow Louise down to the water's edge, but Nick caught her arm.

'So you're not in competition with everyone, then?'

It took Abby two seconds to consider the idea. 'No. Just you.'

Nick chuckled softly and turned, making his way down to the boats, which lay moored and ready to go, while Abby and Louise walked into the water together. It was cool, but not cold. As soon as they started swimming in earnest, Abby knew that she would no longer notice the temperature of the water.

The swimmers lined up at the starting point, flanked by the boats, and on the signal to go, Abby stayed with Louise, slowing her stroke so that the younger woman could keep pace with her. Sunlight glinted on the water. That powerful, joyful feeling as she sliced through the swell and out towards the centre of the lake. The swimmers began to spread out, some ahead of them, and others behind.

Louise was trying too hard to keep up the pace, and Abby dropped back. When Louise realised that she was swimming alone, she began to relax, matching Abby's more leisurely stroke, and the two swam together. Abby found her rhythm and went on to autopilot, selecting a medium-slow song from her mental jukebox and swimming to its beat.

As they rounded the halfway buoy and started on the leg back to the shore, Abby allowed herself a glance at her watch. Thirty minutes. Louise was making good time and they should finish at just over the hour. Slower than Abby could have done, but they weren't racing. All they needed to do was finish the course. She was aware of the support boat, keeping its distance but ready to move in if there were any problems.

Suddenly Louise turned in the water, one hand shooting up. She was in difficulties. Abby stopped, treading water, her own hand up, beckoning the boat in.

'Cramp?' Abby's first reaction was to take hold of Louise and support her in the water. She might still have to do that, but unless it looked as if Louise was going under, she wanted to give her the chance to deal with this herself.

'Y-yes. Whole leg. Frozen.' Louise's eyes were wild, frightened. She was keeping it under control, but only just, and panicking was about the worst thing you could do in open water.

'Okay, steady. Flex your foot.' Abby got a mouthful of water and spat it back out again as the boat eased gently in alongside them. Hopefully, its presence would give Louise some confidence.

She could see Nick, crouched low on the deck, his questioning eyes on her. 'Cramp,' she told him.

'Okay. Louise, relax. Do you want to stop?'

Louise seemed to calm a little at the sound of his voice. 'No. Going off a bit now.'

'Great stuff. Take a few minutes. There's plenty of time.' Nick fixed a cup to the end of the pole that the boats used to pass food and drinks to the swimmers and lowered it to Louise. 'Here. Try and take a few sips.'

The warm drink wouldn't help her straight away, but it was comforting. Louise drank and bobbed up and down in the water beside the boat, easing her leg, for a few minutes. 'Okay. I think I'm good to go now.'

Abby looked up at Nick. He had been quietly assessing the situation, their distance from the shore, the weather, how Louise looked. He gave her one quick nod.

'Stay close to me, then. I'll set the pace.' Abby didn't want Louise to start racing for the shore in a panic. 'We're going to take it easy to start with.'

'Good. We'll move back a bit, but we'll stay well within reach.' Nick was searching Louise's face. The one remaining piece of the puzzle. Whether she had the heart to do it or not. 'If you start to feel any cramping, don't wait and see if it passes but put your hand up immediately. That's an order.'

Apparently 'advice' had fallen by the wayside,

but Nick didn't seem to notice such distinctions. Neither did Louise for that matter, and she gave him a wordless nod, before waving the boat away.

CHAPTER SIX

FORTY minutes later, Louise and Abby climbed out of the water together and onto the jetty. The other swimmers had been watching their progress intently and Louise's crewmates surrounded her as a small round of applause rippled through the other spectators, who had walked down from the field where the fair was underway to see the finish of the swim.

The boat drew alongside the jetty, and Nick climbed off. A quick exchange of words with Louise, his hand on her shoulder in congratulation for a job well done, and he turned and made his way over to where Abby was standing.

'You were in the water too long.' His brow was creased and he almost threw the words at her. Abby wasn't sure what she had been expecting from him, but it wasn't this. She started to walk towards the camper van, where the bag with her clothes was stored, afraid to face him in case he saw her disappointment.

'We finished.'

'Yep. And you have to swim again tomorrow. I'm concerned that if you do all your swims at this pace, you'll wear yourself out.'

She turned, but only so she didn't have to shout over her shoulder at him and run the risk that Louise would hear and take it the wrong way. 'I don't have to. Tomorrow I'll swim on my own.'

'Glad to hear it.' His tone seemed almost mocking, and Abby pushed the towel that he proffered away.

'Okay, then. Just tell me what you would have done?' If he told her that he would have just swum on ahead, leaving Louise to pace herself alone, she was going to laugh in his face.

'I never take my own advice. That's why I'm so marvellously good at giving it.' His tone softened suddenly. 'Come to the van. I'll get you a hot drink.'

He strode away from her, leaning on his stick but barely limping. Abby ignored him and stripped off her wetsuit in one easy motion, born of long practice. The day was warm and sunny but when the breeze touched her skin she began to shiver, goose-bumps rising on her arms.

'Here.' Nick was back again, a steaming mug in one hand, the towel still thrown over his shoulder. 'Take it.'

That was definitely an order. But Abby was cold now, as well as tired and upset, and she took the towel with as good a grace as she could muster, wrapping it around herself. Nick put the drink into her hands before she had a chance to even think about rejecting it, and she sipped it gratefully.

'You're shivering. Come up to the van.' Another order.

'Not if it means that you're going to lecture me.' She may not have much fight left in her at the moment, but she had enough for Nick.

He sighed. 'That was a great swim, Abby.'

'A minute ago you said it was too slow.'

'And it was. But you did it anyway to help a teammate. Come to the van, you're shivering.'

'So I was right, then?' Abby's teeth were chattering but she wasn't moving until he admitted it.

'Yes. Yes, you were right, Abby. Will you come to the van now? Please.'

'Okay.' She couldn't help smiling at his obvious frustration. 'Since you asked nicely.'

Abby let him put his arm loosely around her shoulder and hurry her to the minibus. He opened the back doors and sat her down on the high tailgate. 'Here, let me dry your legs.' He produced another towel and rubbed hard, bringing a little warmth back into her toes, then fetched her bag from inside the vehicle and drew out a pair of warm socks, putting them onto her feet.

That was better. After the slow pace of the swim her body temperature had plummeted, but it seemed to be approaching a more normal level now. Abby wrapped her fingers around the warm mug that he had given her and drained the last of the hot chocolate.

'Right.' He took the mug from her with a grin. 'Let's get you into some warm clothes.'

He didn't give her any time to protest. He lifted her up into the camper van, following and closing the doors behind them. Producing the largest towel she'd ever seen, he wrapped her up in it, rubbing her arms and shoulders to dry her off.

'I'll hold the towel while you get your swimsuit off.' There was a trace of mischief in his voice. Just enough to make Abby's lips begin to quiver into a smile. Not enough to give her any grounds for thinking that the towel wasn't going to stay in place, covering her while she undressed.

'Okay. I'm trusting you, Nick.'

'Good. I'm a very trustworthy person. Only I do have to say that I caught a glimpse of your ankles while I was helping you on with your socks.'

'That's okay. We live in modern times.' He held the towel firmly around her while she wriggled out of her swimsuit.

'Mmm. I'm getting quite inured to the sight of a well-turned ankle. Hardly even give them a second look.' He was grinning broadly, his eyes fixed on the hem of the towel.

'My clothes, Nick.'

'Let's get you dry first.' He rubbed the towel against her back and warmth began to tingle through her. 'There, is that better?' His hands had moved to her hips and the tops of her legs.

Carefully avoiding the sweet, soft places that a lover would touch.

'That's fine.' He needn't have bothered to be so solicitous. Wherever he touched her, even through the thick material of the towel, his hands trailed paths of fire.

'Here's your bag.' He lifted the bag up onto one of the padded seats, seemingly unwilling to go rummaging around in it for her underwear. Perhaps he felt it too. That craving for his skin to touch hers.

'Thanks.' She twisted one arm free of the folds of the towel and Nick awkwardly averted his eyes. Proof positive that he was feeling something. He'd seen her arm before, more times than she could count. As she reached for the bag her forearm brushed against his and he snatched it away. Proof positive times two.

Abby grabbed her underwear and Nick pulled the towel up around her while she put it on. 'Here.' Her thick, cosy sweatpants lay on the top of the pile of clothes and he caught them up and handed them to her.

'Thanks. Can you see a blue sweater in there?'

He hesitated for a moment and then carefully searched in her bag, pulling out her thick sweater and a white T-shirt. 'This what you want?'

Abby took the T-shirt and put it on, and Nick handed her the sweater, turning away to roll her soaking swimsuit in the towel. Then, seemingly at ease with going into her bag now, he pulled out her trainers. 'Sit down.'

Abby sat. In her clothes she felt more at ease. And Nick had been a complete gentleman, even if the thoughts that had been circulating in her head had been less than ladylike. Ignoring the voice at the back of her head that told her she could put her trainers on for herself perfectly well, she held out one foot.

Sitting opposite her, he perched her foot on his knee, easing her shoe on and tying the laces. Then the other. 'Don't do that to me again, Abby.'

'Don't do what?'

'Don't stand there, freezing to death, just to make a point. Next time I start acting like an idiot, feel free to kick my legs out from under me, but then you step over me and go and get yourself warm.'

'Oh, so you're taking it all back now, are you? You only said I was right to get me into the van?' She was trying so hard not to smile, but she could feel her lips twitching.

He grinned, reaching for her mug and refilling it from a Thermos flask, twisting round to sit next to her on the bench. 'Yeah, of course I said it to get you into the van. Doesn't mean I didn't think you *were* right.'

'But under normal circumstances you'd do anything rather than admit it.' Abby took the mug from him and sipped at the smooth, thick chocolate drink.

He chuckled. 'You were right. And I'm sorry. My only defence is that I'm finding it tough, having to sit on the sidelines and worry. I'd rather be swimming.'

'Consider it a learning experience. And you're not doing too badly. I'll give you nine out of ten.' She was goading him now. Nine out of ten was never going to be enough for Nick.

He took the mug from her and set it down on the floor. Those few brief seconds, when his gaze met hers, were enough to burn what was left of Abby's resolve to a cinder.

She almost cried out when his lips brushed hers. That first gentle touch, which sought permission to touch again. And then there was no possibility of anything other than to just keep breathing somehow as he kissed her. Hard, strong and unrelenting. Unlocking the passion that she kept so tightly under control and allowing it to meet his, two fires that burned equally hot.

She could feel his hand, through layers of thick wool and cotton, inching along her ribs. Please. Please, just a little further. His fingers stopped, just short of the soft swell of her breast, and longing exploded deep inside.

'You are so beautiful.' He'd taken his lips from hers to say the words. 'I want more, Abby. I want everything you can give, and then I want to go back and take it all over again.' He left her in little doubt that when that happened it would be eleven out of ten. Or twenty-two if you counted the second time. Abby wanted that too.

'Can I trust you, Nick?'

'You can trust me. Like I said, what happens here stays here.'

That wasn't exactly what she meant. But suddenly she didn't care whether he blew her mind into a million different pieces, took her to places that she'd never been before and couldn't imagine. What he promised was exactly what she wanted.

'Will you think about it, Abby?'

There was nothing to think about, but they couldn't do anything about that here, in a van on a crowded jetty. The trick was going to be contriving to think about something—anything—else in the hours between now and when they could be alone together.

'I'll give it my most careful consideration.'

'Good.' His fingers moved in a soft caress, still just inches short of where she wanted them to be, and she gasped.

'And what about you? Are you thinking about it?' She could hardly get the words out. Hardly bear to hear his answer, in case he wasn't as consumed by this as she was.

'Night and day. I'm very thorough.'

'Hmm. Thorough. Good with ladders.' She planted a kiss on his lips and then drew back again. 'I'm beginning to like you.'

He chuckled. 'That's the plan.'

Nick started as someone banged on the closed doors of the minibus. Probably his guardian angel, saving him from himself before he forgot where he was. Or maybe Abby's. At this point he wasn't sure who needed saving most. Quickly he picked up the mug and put it back into her trembling fingers and then reached back to open the double doors.

'You finished in there?' Louise was standing outside, dressed now, her short dark hair almost dry in the sun.

'Yep. We're done.' Like hell they were. But Abby was warm and dry now, and anything else would have to wait.

'I came to thank Abby for helping me round the course.' Louise craned around him, trying to make eye contact with her new friend, and Nick stepped to one side, feeling suddenly in the way.

Abby shrugged, laughing. 'It's not a competition.'

There it was again. The way she seemed to rub along quite happily with everyone else but him. With him she was fierce, competitive, exasperating. It was driving him crazy and the only way to quell this madness was to pit his strength against hers. Find out how far they could both take things. Then he would be free to leave here and go back to his own, well-ordered, life where nothing was allowed to divert him from his chosen purpose.

'I raised five hundred pounds today.' Louise climbed up into the van and plumped herself down next to Abby. 'Only my parents threw in a hundred, so really it's only four.'

'It's great that they're supporting you like this.' She said it without even a flicker of resentment. It had to be pure generosity of spirit that allowed her to be pleased for Louise when she'd clearly had precious little parental support of her own.

'Yeah, s'pose so. They've always been good like that.'

'It means a lot.' Abby shook her head abruptly, her corn-coloured hair spilling around her shoulders. 'Come on. Let's go see what they're doing at the fun day.'

By the time they reached the field, where the fun day had already got off to a noisy start, their little group had swollen to a small crowd. Jokes rippling back and forth. Laughter. The palpable relief that the first leg of the swim had gone well and everyone had shown that the months of planning and training hadn't gone to waste. Louise professed a wish to have her fortune told and dragged a couple of her crewmates along with her into the brightly decorated tent.

'Not going to see what's in your future?' Abby had hung back, next to Nick.

'Nope. I already know.'

'Got it all planned out, have you?' Her pale blue eyes, almost translucent in the sunlight, gave the lie to that. He hadn't planned on this.

'More or less. Inasmuch as you can plan anything.'

'But things don't always go to plan.'

The fall, which had first injured his knee and marred a career that had until then been unstoppable. The drugs. Helen leaving him. Just one slip had brought the house of cards that he'd called his life, cascading down on him and plunging him into another existence, one where he'd said and done things that he could never forgive himself for.

'No, they don't. But if you don't have a plan, there's nothing to work your way back to when things go bad.'

Concern flickered in her eyes. 'Is that what you did, Nick? Worked your way back to the original plan?'

She had seen the thing that it had taken him months to divine. 'No. The thing about drugs is that getting clean is just the first step. You need to work through the issues that made you drug dependent in the first place as well.'

'I imagine that's the toughest part.'

'One of them.' He'd understood the issues and worked through them, but that hadn't absolved him from the shame of what he'd done. 'We see a lot in our jobs, Abby, yours and mine. I couldn't deal with failure, with what I did not being enough. When I was injured, I couldn't deal with not being able to will myself better.'

She shrugged. 'Who can?'

'True. But it became everything to me. I drove myself too hard, took responsibility for things I couldn't change and in the end that broke me.' Nick's heart was thumping in his chest. He was saying too much. How could he imagine that Abby should understand?

'Saving the world's such a great idea. Just as long as you know you can't do it, and it doesn't blind you to the things you can do.' She was smiling ruefully.

'Yeah.' He shrugged. 'But things are different now. I'm the one in control.'

She looked at him thoughtfully, as if she was about to disagree with him. Nick felt the hairs on the back of his neck prickle at the thought. Disagreeing with Abby was like making love.

She opened her mouth for the first caress, and suddenly their attention was caught by the loudspeaker system. *'Dr Maitland to the Medical Tent, please.'*

'Wh—? Where's the medical tent?' She swung round, scanning the field.

'Over there.' Nick pointed to the tent in the far

corner of the field and she hesitated. Catching her hand, he led her across the rough ground at the briskest trot he could manage.

Pete met them at the entrance to the tent. 'Glad you're here. We have a boy, seven years old, who seems to be having some kind of fit. The parents are here. He's awake, but he seems very drowsy and disoriented. We've called an ambulance, but it'll be a little while.'

The tent was full of people, talking quietly, waiting around to see if they could be of help. Abby was looking at them, her hands clasped together tightly. 'Thanks, Pete. I'll take it from here. I need to find the first-aid kit and get some of these people out of here.'

She'd either forgotten or was ignoring the fact that she didn't have to do this all by herself. Nick leaned over towards her. 'You concentrate on the boy. I'll deal with everything else.' He took her arm and eased through the crowd, making a space for Abby to kneel down next to a camp bed that contained the prone figure of a child. Leaving her to it, he turned.

'Can we have some room, please? Thanks, everyone, the doctor's here and she needs everyone to stand back.'

The crowd began to disperse. Out of the corner of his eye Nick could see Abby beginning to carefully examine the boy, and he grabbed the bulky medical kit, setting it down next to her.

'Thanks.' She was calm now. Steady as a rock. 'Perhaps if everyone who isn't able to help could wait outside…'

Nick began to usher the concerned onlookers out of the tent. He stationed one of the organisers next to the entrance, with instructions that only emergencies should enter, and hurried back to her side.

'So you found him lying on the ground?' She was trying to get some sense from the boy's crying mother. 'Whereabouts?'

'He'd just been playing on the bouncy castle. It was right behind there.'

'Okay.' Abby had her fingers on the boy's pulse and swivelled round towards Nick. 'Where's the generator? Could he have got to it?'

He could see where she was headed. Pete's suddenly pale face confirmed it. What if the boy had somehow managed to get close enough to the generator to get an electric shock from it?

'It's unlikely. But we'll check.' Nick didn't have to look for Sam. He'd been his second-in-command for long enough now that each knew where the other was by instinct. 'Sam, take someone and check that the generator's still secure, will you?'

'If my kid's been injured by negligence, you'll be hearing a great deal more of this. Where's this bloody generator?' The boy's father was on his feet, face red, fists clenched by his sides.

Abby ignored him completely, but Nick could see tension in her face as she tried to concentrate on what she was doing. Quickly he drew the boy's father to one side.

'Look, I know this is difficult, but your son's conscious and he can hear what's going on around him. You need to let him know that you're here for him and that he's going to be okay.'

'Right, and while I'm doing that, you lot could be covering up whatever's happened to him. Not bloody likely.'

'There's not going to be any cover-up. We need

to find out what happened so that the doctor can do the right thing for your son. You need to be with your family.' Nick almost snarled the words at the man. He could understand his anger, his helplessness. But this wasn't helping anyone.

'Fair enough. But I'm not going to let this go if it turns out that there has been some sort of negligence.'

'Neither am I.' Nick hoped to hell there hadn't been. Pete had two daughters of his own, as well as grandchildren. He was always a stickler for safety and he would never forgive himself if a child had been injured through any oversight of his.

The man nodded briefly and then turned to sit by his wife's side, one arm around her shoulders and his other hand covering his son's. Abby's brief glance at Nick said it all. *Thanks. Way to go.*

'Has he been a bit off colour recently? Listless, more sleepy than normal? Maybe he's complained of headaches or disturbance in his vision?' She turned to the mother again.

'A little drowsy maybe. He didn't want to come out this afternoon, he was holed up in his bedroom, watching TV, but I didn't think anything of it.' Tears began to roll down the woman's face.

'Okay. That's fine. His breathing and heartbeat are both steady. His temperature's normal.' Abby looked down again as her young charge began to stir restlessly. 'I'm just going to sit him up.'

Gently she cradled the boy in one arm and lifted him up into a sitting position. The child was starting to retch and Abby just managed to tip the contents from a container behind her and hold it in front of him, before he vomited.

'Okay. You're fine. Better out than in, eh?' She was smiling down at the boy, whose eyes were now resolutely closed. Nick took the container from her and pushed a paper napkin into her hand, and she wiped the boy's mouth. 'Can you hear me, Ethan?'

Ethan moaned and thrashed weakly in her arms. 'I know. You don't feel well. I'm a doctor, Ethan, and I'm here to help you. Can you open your eyes for me?'

The boy's eyes fluttered open.

'Good. That's great, Ethan, well done. Look, your mum and dad are right here.'

'Hey, there, Ethan.' His mother summoned a smile from the unending reservoir that parents seemed to keep for their children. 'You had us worried for a moment there, but you look much better now.' She turned to Abby, gratitude glistening in her eyes. 'Can I give him some water?'

'Just let him rinse his mouth out for the time being.' She gave Ethan's mother an encouraging smile and Nick felt his lips twitch in response. He was proud of Abby. The only thing that held her back was that sometimes she seemed to doubt her own abilities.

He turned in response to a touch on his arm. 'Sam. What's the story?'

'The generator enclosure is secure. Jim and I checked it out thoroughly and there's no way a fly could get in there.' Nick breathed a sigh of relief and nodded quickly towards Pete. The older man got the message and seemed to breathe again.

'Find anything else out?'

'Yeah. One of the kids that was playing in that area saw him go down. He said that he seemed quite normal and then suddenly he was on the ground. They didn't see anything hit him, he just crumpled.'

'Have you left Jim there?'

'Yep. Just in case.'

'Good job. Thanks, Sam.' Nick made his way to Abby's side, relaying the information to her quietly, and she nodded in acknowledgement.

'Okay.' She pressed her lips together in thought, looking up as a couple of ambulancemen walked into the tent. 'Will you make sure his mother keeps him sitting up in case he's sick again? I'll go and speak to these guys. Call me if he seems suddenly drowsy or disoriented, or there's anything else that worries you.'

She went to meet the ambulance crew, talking quickly to them as they made their way over. 'I'll go with you to the hospital…' She watched as the boy was lifted gently onto a stretcher and then drew his father to one side, talking to him quietly.

She turned to Nick, standing close, her voice low. 'I've just told the father that I think Ethan may have had an epileptic fit. He's given me permission to tell you, because if I'm right then there's nothing that Pete or anyone else could have done to prevent it.' Her fingers skimmed the front of Nick's shirt and he allowed himself to clasp them briefly.

'Thanks.'

'Got to go.'

'Right. Later, Abby.'

CHAPTER SEVEN

ABBY floated quietly in the hotel swimming pool. It wasn't big enough to do more than just drift and enjoy the feeling of weightlessness that being in the water gave her, but she could see the sky through the glass panels in the ceiling and she could feel herself beginning to relax. Pete had made an appearance at the hospital and when he'd heard that Ethan was doing well and that there was nothing more either of them could do had brought Abby back to the hotel. She'd eaten, spent a little while on her bed, trying to read, and then been drawn to the water while she waited for Nick to return.

'Here you are.' Nick's voice cut through her thoughts. The ones that were largely centred around him anyway.

'You're back. Been working?' He was wearing long, work-worn shorts and a T-shirt, his already tanned skin still glowing with the heat of the afternoon sun.

'Yep. The kit's all stowed and the guys will take the tents and infrastructure down tomorrow. Woe betide anyone who touches it without Pete being there.' He kicked off his deck shoes and sat down at the side of the pool, dangling his legs in the water, and Abby let herself float towards him.

'What's with the new knee support?' He wasn't wearing the heavy brace that Abby had given him, but a lighter one, less bulky.

'Dr Patel said I could try this one out. It's a bit less cumbersome. How did things go at the hospital?'

'They agreed it was probably an epileptic fit. They'll have to do some tests.' She rolled onto her face in the water and then round onto her back again. 'I was hoping I might have been wrong.'

'You wanted to be wrong?' He raised one eyebrow. Almost a challenge, but not quite.

'Epilepsy's going to have an impact on Ethan's life. I'd rather it was something a little less serious.'

'At least it wasn't anything more serious.'

'The glass is half-full, you mean.'

'He's okay and getting the treatment he needs. I'd say it was a good deal more than half-full.' He grinned crookedly. 'You were there when he needed help.'

'Hmm. I was…' Abby had been out of her depth. Faced with a situation that was outside her speciality and beyond her experience.

'You were what?'

'Afraid.' The admission slipped out before Abby had a chance to jam the cork back into the bottle. 'I don't know how I would have handled the situation if you hadn't been there.'

'It wasn't your job to handle the situation. It was your job to give Ethan medical help.'

'Yes, but…' Nick had needed to step in and deal with the crowd of people in the medical tent and with Ethan's father. She hadn't been in control and, even though he hadn't rebuked her for it, Nick must have seen it.

'What was that piece of wisdom you offered up this morning?' He stopped for a moment in mock thought. 'About how not being able to save the world shouldn't blind you to the things you can do?'

'You were listening, then.'

'I always listen. You should try it some time.' He chuckled as Abby directed a splash of water at him. 'Seriously, though, you did what you were trained for, which was to diagnose and treat. Ethan was lucky to have you there.'

Nick's praise made her toes curl with pleasure. 'It's nice of you to say so.'

He gave a little gesture of frustration. 'This is the first time you've had to deal with serious injury outside the hospital environment?'

'Yes.' Did it really show that much?

'Give yourself a break. You did fine. You can't do everything on your own. That was one of the first things I learned when I joined the fire service.'

'Don't you ever feel afraid, though?'

'What, sending men into a burning building? Going in myself?' He shrugged. 'I'd be crazy not to. Fear can be positive as well as negative, it helps us gauge risk.'

'That's not what I meant.' The water in the pool

lapped gently against the blue and white tiles that surrounded it. Fear seemed a very long way away here.

'What else do I have to be afraid of?'

'There's always something.' Like losing control. Nick had pretty much admitted to that already.

'*You* frighten me.'

'What?' Abby lunged backwards in the water, away from him.

'Yep. Gonna have to do something about that.' Mischief ignited in his dark eyes and desire stirred in the pit of her stomach. Slowly, almost as if time was obliging enough to allow her a few extra seconds to savour the action, he drew his T-shirt over his head then slipped into the pool, shorts and all, and took a few languorous strokes. Dived, swimming underneath her, and then surfaced next to her. 'Definitely going to have to do something.'

'Oh, so the great Nick Hunter can't be afraid of a woman, is that it?'

'Yeah, that's about the size of it.' He slid one arm around her waist, pulling her in, and Abby almost forgot to breathe. 'Only one thing to do when you're afraid of something.'

'Face it head on.' She was trembling now. He must feel it, her fingers fluttering uncertainly on his back and sliding across his powerful shoulders. 'Look it straight in the eye.'

He kissed her and they sank together, water closing over their heads. Small bubbles skittered to the surface and he held the kiss for long moments, before launching them both upwards again. They broke the surface together, lungs sucking in air, their bodies pressed together in the water.

'We're both adults, Abby. We can do as we please. We don't need to make any promises or have any expectations. We could just do whatever feels right.'

Whatever felt right. Was it really that easy? Right now it felt as if it might be. Maybe she should try the unexpected for once in her life. Abby was used to making a cool-headed decision about a man. Choosing someone who would fit into her routine and leave it undisturbed. Nick didn't even come close to fitting that description.

'Kiss me again.'

'Thought you'd never ask.' For once Nick did as he was told.

'You taste of chlorine.'

He grinned at her. 'So do you. Want to take a shower?'

'Yeah. Want to join me?'

Abby made to back him towards the pool steps but he stopped her. 'There's no good time to mention this. In case you were wondering how to ask, I have some condoms in my room.'

'Good.' That was a weight off her mind. Now she wouldn't have to admit that she'd bought some that afternoon. 'Thank you, Nick.' She wound her arms around his neck. 'I really appreciate that you…thought about everything.'

'Can I stop now? Thinking about everything?'

'Please do.'

By the time they'd got out of the pool, wrapped towels around themselves and Nick had hurried Abby up the back stairs to his room, she was shivering. He ushered her inside, dropping his keys onto the small occasional table by the door.

'Wow! A four-poster.' Nick's room was in the

oldest part of the hotel building and unlike hers, which was bright, modern and largely unremarkable, it was charmingly old-fashioned. The large bed, complete with heavy brocade curtains, dominated the room.

'Yeah.' Nick was busy, tracing his fingers across her shoulders, and he didn't even glance at it. 'Mrs Pearce says that Henry VIII slept in that bed.'

'Really? I'm not sure I'd like to sleep in Henry VIII's bed.' Who was she trying to kid? Nick had a much more recent claim on it. And his chocolate suede eyes promised so very much.

'Actually, it's Victorian.' He reached up and thumped one of the beams above his head, his gaze still locked with hers. 'So are these, they're not structural. Mock Tudor.'

'Oh. Good.'

'Now that we have that out of the way, can I show you the shower?' He grinned wickedly, and began to back her slowly towards the bathroom.

The door slammed behind them and hot water began to cascade downwards, pushing steam into the room. The towel around his waist crumpled onto the floor, closely followed by his shorts. Abby gasped with admiration. He was beautiful. And for the moment he was all hers.

'Let me.' Her trembling fingers had moved to unfasten the towel she had wrapped firmly around herself, but his were there first. Gently pulling it from around her body. Drawing the straps of her swimming costume from her shoulders and rolling it down until it was around her waist.

She wanted to feel her skin against his, and when she clung to him a long, low sigh escaped his lips. He kissed her again, moulding her body against his until even that wasn't enough.

'Nick.'

He knew what she wanted. But he seemed to enjoy her agonies of impatience, slowly pulling her swimming costume down further until she could step out of it.

'Put your hair up.' His fingers found the elastic tie, still looped around her wrist from where she'd loosened her hair after she'd taken off her swimming cap. Abby twisted her hair onto the top of her head, securing it firmly.

A low growl of approval escaped his throat. 'I never knew that a woman fixing her hair could be so seductive.'

His words made her feel bold. He had seemed to sense that this was not something she usually did and the tremble of his limbs, so obviously wanting her but trying to go slowly, gave Abby confidence. She pulled him into the shower, picking up the soap and slowly lathering his chest.

'Two can play at that game.' He squeezed her hand, making the soap slip through her fingers, and caught it with his other hand.

The water beat down onto his back as he began to soap her body. Starting with her arms and working up to her shoulders. Slowly. Deliberately. Abby shuddered with the promise of where his hands would go next. He lingered over her breasts and she cried out. Made his way down her ribcage and Abby hung onto him for dear life.

It had to be now. He was as ready for her as she was for him. She'd never made love in a shower before. Abby's fingers found one of the grab rails and closed tightly around it.

'Steady.' His fingers were inching downwards,

gently stroking, stoking the fire in her belly. 'Hang on there, sweetheart. We have a way to go yet.'

'I can't, Nick.' She was almost pleading with him. Abby didn't know how much more of this she could handle.

'Sure you can. The higher we climb, the harder we fall. But I'll be there to catch you, I promise.'

Something broke. Her will. Her resolve to stay strong. She didn't care any more if she was weak, crying in his arms. As long as he just kept hold of her. 'Don't let me go, Nick.'

'I won't.' His voice was low, almost guttural. 'I can't, not now.'

Nick wanted to hoist her up onto his arms and carry her to the bed, but he wasn't sure whether his leg would take the extra weight. The gesture would almost certainly be ruined if he fell flat on his face and crushed her into the bargain. Instead, he guided her gently, their motion almost that of a slow dance, holding her tight against his raging body. Too much more of this and he was going to black out from sheer, frustrated need.

He'd sensed he should go slowly, but how much longer he could keep this up was anyone's guess.

The answer came back immediately. As long as it took. From her reaction to him, she wasn't used to a man taking his time. Maybe he could show her something different.

He guided her to the bed and lifted her onto it, lying down beside her. Unfastening her hair, he watched almost mesmerised as it spilled back down across her shoulders. Nick meant the kiss to be tender, reassuring, but somehow his hunger broke through, meeting joyfully with hers, leaving them both breathless.

She was moving against him, the delicious friction of her skin driving him crazy. Rolling her over onto her back, he parted her legs, his fingers searching for that sweet spot, hoping that she would cry out when he found it.

She did, and then again when he moved to slide one finger inside her. Almost as soon as he did so, he felt her muscles tighten and quiver, just for a moment, and her eyes widened in surprise.

He kissed her flushed cheek and moved his fingers again, making her gasp. Nick knew what to do now. Slowly, he pushed her higher, controlling the pace, until finally she broke. Her cry of disbelief turned to one of sheer pleasure as her body convulsed in time with the movement of his fingers. She was, for this moment, entirely his and more beautiful than he could ever have imagined.

He held her tightly while her body relaxed into his, stubbornly telling himself that if she wanted to curl up and sleep now, that would be okay. He could deal with it. Maybe chopping his arm off would take his mind off the urgent, almost deafening clamour that echoed through every part of his body.

'Now you,' she whispered shyly into his chest. Nick hesitated. Was his own need blinding him, making him believe that this was what she really wanted?

'I said, now you.' Her voice was steadier now, more assured, and she disentangled herself from his embrace and sat up. Ran one finger from the mid-point of his chest downwards.

'Abby…' Her name was the only thing in his

head. The one word that summed up everything he wanted.

'We're not done yet.' She bent over him, whispering into his ear. Took his hand and guided it slowly across her body. Her low moan of arousal almost broke him.

Eager to do her bidding, he shifted across the bed, pulling the drawer of the bedside table open and tipping half the contents unheeded onto the floor as he groped for the packet of condoms. Nick made himself concentrate on rolling the condom down into place. No mistakes. Then he was free again, free to enjoy the way she caught her breath, eyes bright with expectation, as he rolled her over onto her back, settling his hips between her legs.

'Is this what you want?' He let her anticipate what he was about to do for a moment, before he slid inside her. Not too far. He wanted to make this last.

'Is that all you have?' The smile on her face was downright wicked and she twisted her hips, sending shivers of delight through his body. What on earth had made him think that he was in control here?

'Nope.' Another inch, and his head began to swim.

Then she did it. Raised her hips off the bed, wrapping her legs around his waist, taking him in deep. The realisation that this was the only place he needed to be hit him like a sledgehammer and when she kissed him, his control broke. He didn't just want her, he needed her. Her body joined with his. Breathing as if they were one. Each movement he made sending pleasure surging through them both.

He had no idea how long he managed to hold on. How did you measure time when each moment was everything? And however long it was, it was enough, complete and perfect. When the sweet, head-spinning convulsions of her muscles sent him over the edge he was lost, falling wildly, with only Abby to catch him.

CHAPTER EIGHT

ABBY woke, to find Nick's arms around her, his body spooning hers. Not a dream, then.

Tentatively, she moved one arm. Cleared her throat. Nick's breathing didn't falter. He must be asleep. Trying not to look at him, she eased herself away from him and got out of the bed.

'Where are you going?'

'What? I thought you were asleep.' In the soft light of a lamp glowing in the corner of the room Abby could see him propped up on one arm in the bed.

'I was watching you sleep.' He almost sounded embarrassed, as if he'd been caught taking the last chocolate from the box.

'What's the time?'

'Half past nine.'

'I suppose we've missed dinner, then.'

He chuckled. 'Yes. But Mrs P. told me the other

day where the key to the kitchen is kept. I have permission to make sandwiches.'

Abby supposed that the very grin she was getting now had charmed that concession out of Mrs Pearce. 'I'll, um, go to my room and get dressed and see you down there, then.'

'Won't you stay here?' The way he was looking at her was making her tremble. She could deal with him wanting her, he could hardly want her any more than she wanted him. But the tenderness. The intimacy, which had provoked a response from deep inside her. That she wasn't used to and she hadn't banked on it happening for the first time with Nick.

He was already out of bed, pulling on jeans and a T-shirt then shooting her a grin and a wink around the closing door. Before she quite knew what she was doing, Abby grinned back and blew him a kiss.

She flipped the overhead lights on, trailing into the bathroom and squeezing out her sopping-wet swimming costume in the shower. Straightening the towels that had been flung onto the rack. Shivering slightly in the cool evening air. Smiling.

Abby couldn't think about all they'd done together. What he'd made her feel. The way she'd let go of everything, craving only his touch. Belonging to him alone and feeling things that only he could make her feel.

'Don't hold back, Nick.' She wondered whether it had sounded like the plea it had been. Whether he knew that she'd begged.

He must have known. That sudden grin, the one that made her stomach flip just to think about it. *'It's not a race, sweetheart. I'm planning on coming last.'* Despite herself, Abby found herself smiling again.

By the time he returned, balancing a tray in one hand, the tracksuit she'd left down by the pool tucked under his arm, she was back in the big bed. Knees tucked up to her chin, the covers wrapped around her like a shield. Some hope. Just seeing him again made her heart pump a little faster.

He put her tracksuit down on a chair in the corner of the room and then brought the tray over to the bed, setting it down. 'Here.' Pulling his T-shirt off, he handed it to her. 'Is this enough to coax you out of there?'

Abby slipped the T-shirt over her head, sliding out from under the covers, and he nodded his approval. 'That's better.'

She watched, as he strode over to the fireplace, finding a box of matches on the mantelpiece and lighting the candles that stood there. Flipping the lights off, he returned to the bedside.

'If we have a four-poster, we may as well enjoy it.' His eyes twinkled in the soft candlelight as he loosed the curtains and drew them around her, leaving only the side that faced the fireplace open.

'Mmm. This is nice. Like our own little hidey-hole, away from the world. Come inside.' Abby patted the space next to her on the bed.

They ate ravenously, and when Abby had collected the cups and plates back onto the tray he folded her in a lazy, satisfied embrace. Until then, Abby had always found some excuse to skip this comfortable companionability after sex. Having to leave because she'd needed to be up early in the morning. Rolling over to sleep because she'd been tired. None of that was ever going to wash with Nick. His bed wasn't just a place for sleeping and making love, it was a playground, where anything might happen.

'I don't really know that much about you.' The observation escaped her before she had time to think about it.

He chuckled, tracing his finger along her arm. 'What more do you want?'

'Oh, the usual things.' There was so much more to Nick than she had thought when she had first met him. She wanted to know everything. Every last detail. 'You were born…?'

'Yep. Can't tell you much about that, you'd have to ask my mother. One brother, one sister. Aunts and uncles, nephews and nieces. All the usual suspects.'

'You have nephews and nieces?'

'Yep. Four in all.'

'But you never had any children yourself?' Abby didn't even know that about him. Whether there was a broken relationship in his past. A child maybe.

'No. That didn't happen. I thought it might, at one point, but...' He shook his head ruefully. 'I put paid to that.'

'How so?'

'It wasn't exactly my finest hour.' She felt his body tense against hers slightly, and he changed the subject too quickly. 'What about you?'

'Me? There's nothing very interesting about me.'

'I find you fascinating. So far I know that you were bullied as a child. There's a lot more to you than that.'

Abby smiled against his chest. 'Yes, there is. The bullying's just the bad stuff. I left that behind a long time ago.' The therapy had helped. Getting older had helped, along with the swimming. All that was left was a sense of regret that things had not been different. 'It took a while. For a long time I used to find out whatever I could about the boys who had bullied me. I think I was waiting for them to get what I considered were their just deserts.'

He curled around her protectively, his eyes flashing dark and dangerous. 'So who were they?

Names and addresses will do. I'll take it from there.'

He was only half joking. Nick wouldn't do anything, but it didn't stop him from wanting to, and Abby was irrationally grateful for that. 'You will not. It took me years to get to the point of not caring about them any more, and I'm not going back there now.' She reached to brush her fingers against his lips. 'Sometimes these things are better left in the past.'

'Sometimes.' He seemed to be considering the idea. Almost tempted by it.

'So you know my darkest secrets. What about yours?' The challenge was laid gently before him, rather than being flung at his feet. If he didn't want to talk about it, that was okay.

Nick shrugged. 'Addicts can be self-absorbed, blind and cruel. I was all of those things. I was living with someone, but she left me. She was right to do so.'

Abby couldn't believe that, but Nick seemed so certain. 'How did you get involved with drugs? If you don't mind me asking.'

He reached for her, holding her close, as if for comfort. 'I don't mind.' He fell silent.

'Do you mind answering?' she cajoled gently. If Nick didn't want to answer, she knew he wouldn't, but maybe he needed to find some way of talking about it.

He sighed, pulling himself upright against the pillows that were piled at the head of the bed. 'When I first injured my knee, I tore the cartilage badly. After the operation I developed a Baker's cyst, which went unnoticed until it burst.'

Abby flinched. She wasn't in a consulting room now, and that was allowed.

'Yeah.' He grinned. 'It hurt. I was desperate to get back to work, and I thought that taking more and more painkillers would get me back on my feet sooner. I played one doctor off against another and got duplicate prescriptions. By the time I resorted to the internet, it wasn't about the pain, it was all about wanting more of the drugs.'

Abby nodded. 'And the woman you were living with?'

Nick sighed. 'I kept all of this from Helen. I started going out alone, without telling her where

I was going, and even when I was at home I wasn't really there for her. She knew that something was up and thought I was seeing someone else.'

'Were you?'

'In a way I was. The drugs had become the other woman. But I let her go on believing that I was cheating on her so that she wouldn't find out what I was really doing. I let her go through all of that hurt and then walk away from me because I cared more about the drugs than I did her.'

A pulse beat at the side of his brow. If she slapped him now, Abby knew that he wouldn't flinch, that he'd simply take it as a small part of what he deserved.

'Did you ever tell her?' Perhaps Nick's insistence that their relationship was only temporary was because he had unfinished business elsewhere. The thought made Abby feel sick.

'Yes. After I got clean, I went to see her, explained everything. She didn't forgive me, but she understood. By then she had a new partner.' Nick shrugged. 'Even I could see that he made her happier than I ever did.'

'And…and you?' Abby clasped her hands together tightly to stop them from shaking.

'It's over, Abby. Helen and I were never right for each other. It was one of those things that shouldn't have been in the first place.' He laid his hand on hers. 'Believe me.'

That was something. Abby tried not to heave a sigh of relief. 'But you still feel that you let her down?'

'I didn't treat her as I should have. It doesn't make any difference that things turned out for the best. I've been trying all my life not to be the kind of man who puts an addiction above the people he should be caring for and protecting, and I failed.'

Abby took a deep breath and went for the fifty-thousand-dollar question. 'Who was that man? The one you've been trying not to be.'

He looked at her for long moments, before dropping his gaze to where his finger slowly traced around the pattern of the bedspread. 'My father. He was an alcoholic. He left us when I was eight and that was the best thing he ever did for any of us. It was hard for my mother, alone with three kids, but not as bad as when he was around.'

'But…but you're not like that, Nick.'

'I'm just like him. He was always sorry when he lashed out at my mother. But it was never enough to make him stop.'

'But you kicked the drugs.'

He shook his head. 'Even Helen leaving wasn't enough to make me give up. I did the unforgiveable and went back to work, just on desk duties, but I still shouldn't have done it. I was planning out a training exercise and didn't bother to check everything because I was strung out, wanting to get home. Luckily someone else did and found a faulty piece of equipment that could have put lives at risk.'

'You got help then?'

'Ted Bishop was my station commander back then. I went to him, told him everything, and offered to resign. He threw it back in my face and challenged me to take the harder option. I took him up on it, took a leave of absence and got myself clean. I'll always be thankful to him for that.'

'So the fire service knows? About your history.'

'Only those who need to. Ted had to put it through channels to get me the help I needed so it's on my record, but everyone else thought that I'd re-injured my knee. I didn't have the spine to tell them any different.'

'You had the guts to do something about it. To turn your life around.' Abby hated it that Nick talked about himself like this. Spineless was the last description that anyone could apply to him. If anything, he had a bit too much spine at times.

His fingers slid across the bedspread towards hers and then stopped short of them. It was as if he no longer felt he had the right to touch her. 'I'm sorry, Abby. I shouldn't have told you about this. Not tonight.'

Abby knew why he'd told her. She'd asked. The intimacy between them had stripped him of his protective shell, and when she'd asked he'd found a way to answer. And she could feel that those answers had driven a wedge between them, reminding him of all the reasons why he believed they couldn't be together.

He swung his legs over the side of the bed, sitting up and rubbing his face. 'You should get some sleep, Abby. You're swimming tomorrow.'

'Yeah, probably.' She laid her cheek against his back, winding her arms around him. 'Will you hold me, Nick?'

'Don't you want to go back to your own room to sleep?'

'No. Why, are you trying to get rid of me?' Maybe he wasn't ready to leave his past behind yet. Another time perhaps. But she wasn't going to let him get away with thinking that he was right about himself, by allowing him to chase her away.

He turned, rolling her with him back onto the bed. 'Come here.'

Day Two. Coniston Water. Three miles.

Nick sat on the deck of the boat, watching as Abby sliced into the choppy water. He'd resisted the temptation to wake her in the night and make love to her again. And this morning he'd let her dress quickly and slip from his room, before the rest of the team stirred. Just a smile and a kiss. Nothing more, however much he wanted it.

She seemed stronger than usual, though. Her stroke was confident, economical. She'd taken the lead almost immediately and Nick had steered the support boat after her, signalling to the other boats to stay back and watch over the rest of the swimmers.

'She's a good girl.' Pete was behind him, and Nick didn't turn to acknowledge his words, keeping his eye fixed on Abby. 'She'll do the whole course in under an hour thirty if she keeps this up.'

'I just hope she doesn't tire herself.' Nick's neck began to burn. Swimming wasn't the only physical activity that Abby had been up to in the last twenty-four hours and he was the one who would be to blame if she began to flag.

'She'll be all right.' Pete seemed to have nothing to base the supposition on other than instinct, but Nick knew enough to trust Pete's gut. He'd done it enough times before Pete had retired, and it had never let him down.

'I hope so.'

Pete let out a short, barking laugh. 'Stop worrying. I hope you're not like this when you're around her.'

Nick went to deny everything, and then realised he didn't have a clue what Pete was talking about. 'Like what?'

'Jittery, mate. She won't sink if you take your eyes off her, you know.'

'I know. I'm just studying her stroke. Looking for irregularities.'

'That's what they call it these days, is it? Does she know?'

Nick turned to Pete in exasperation. 'Know what?'

'Something tells me there's something going on between you two. And you don't have much of a reputation for sticking with a relationship.' Pete's shrewd blue eyes were fixed on Nick.

'You think I'd hurt her?'

'That's up to you. If you did, I'd be sorry to see it.' Pete regarded him thoughtfully. 'I'd be sorry for you, too.'

There was no point in asking Pete what he knew or how he knew it. He'd just make some oblique comment about listening to his gut and let the matter slide. 'It's a holiday thing, Pete. We both know it. I won't make promises to her that I can't keep.'

'And why can't you keep them?'

Pete may have made a few lucky guesses, but he didn't have all the answers. Abby had heard the worst about him from his own lips. Even if she'd had the goodness of heart not to reject him straight away, she must understand now why it was better for both of them if this was a purely temporary arrangement.

'It's a crease in time, Pete—' Nick didn't get a chance to finish. A cry from the water made him whirl round, his knee suddenly giving out. Nick stumbled, landing awkwardly on the deck.

'Watch it!' Abby was treading water by the side of the boat, grinning.

'What's the matter?'

'Nothing. Just wondered what you two were up to. I was feeling a bit neglected.' There was a playful tone to her voice, different from her usual grim determination. And she seemed entirely unaware that she had stopped and that the swimmers behind her were beginning to gain on her.

Nick resumed his position at the side of the boat. 'Just keep swimming, will you? Look, the others are catching up.'

She laughed. 'Thought this wasn't a race.' Before he could answer, she had turned, soft sheets of water streaming across her rolling body, and started swimming again, striking out strongly for the shore and the end of the course.

Nick was there for her when she got out of the water, and when she'd stripped off her wetsuit she let him wrap her in a towel. He loved doing things for her. Taking her swim hat, when she pulled it off her head, shaking her hair free. Handing her a hot drink from the van.

She was bright, almost elated. 'That was fun. I could do it again...'

'Well, your wish is granted.' He liked granting her wishes, too. 'Tomorrow...'

'Buttermere.' She regarded the sky, an inferior blue to her eyes but cloudless all the same. 'Think the weather will hold?'

'The forecast's good.'

'Well, fingers crossed. I'll just go and get changed and then watch the others come in.'

He left her to it. She seemed bright, strong. More in charge of herself than he'd ever seen her. Being here, taking part in the swimming was obviously doing her good and he should give her some space, let her enjoy it to the full. He could only weigh her down, hold her back.

When she re-emerged, dressed in warm clothes, and ran down to the water's edge, ready to cheer the other swimmers to the finish line, he didn't follow. A few hours out of the circle of delight that she seemed to carry with her wherever she went would do them both good.

CHAPTER NINE

'WHERE have you been?' Nick sauntered into the dining room and sat down at Abby's table as if nothing had happened. She had already decided not to wait for him any longer and was tucking into her evening meal. She'd decided not to ask him where he'd been, too.

'I...' The slight hesitation told her that he'd stayed away on purpose. 'I went to see Ted Bishop.'

Abby flashed him a brittle smile. She'd thought that yesterday afternoon might have changed things. But knowing what had made Nick into the man he was hadn't suddenly turned him into someone different. It had just cleared up a few of the questions that had been outstanding in her mind. 'About the arson attacks? I thought that you'd finished with your input on that.'

'I dropped in and took him to lunch and we had a chat about the new job I've been offered.'

'What did he say?' Abby kept eating while Nick ordered his meal. She didn't want to hear what had kept him away for the rest of the afternoon. It was probably something trivial, and then she was going to have to resent him for it.

'I did most of the talking, actually. Told him what you'd said and he just nodded sagely.'

Abby felt her shoulders relax, and she laid her knife and fork down with a clatter. Nick did this every time. Getting angry with him was a lot easier when he wasn't around than when he was sitting right next to her.

'So he's persuaded you. That it's what you really want.'

'No. You persuaded me. It was good to hear myself say it, though, and find that I really believed it.'

Pleasure leaked into her fingertips, and she flexed her hands impatiently. This was Nick all over. Charming, tantalising and cruelly honest about the fact that ultimately he didn't belong to her. It wasn't what he wanted, and Abby reminded herself that it wasn't what she wanted either. She didn't want to be the clingy girlfriend, devastated whenever he decided not to tell her where he was going or what he was doing. That wasn't what they'd both signed up for here.

'We spent some time going over the case as well.' He grinned. 'Ted can do with the help, so we broke the rules. Just for the afternoon.'

Not as trivial as she'd thought. Warmth began to permeate the protective layer that Abby had wrapped around herself for comfort. 'How's it going?'

'They're making some progress. The profile has helped, and I've suggested that there could be a grudge involved in selecting the targets. All the fires seem to be aimed at places of authority—a school, a driving test centre and so on.'

'So it's not just someone who likes to light fires then stand around and watch the damage they're doing?'

'It probably is. But where he's lighting the fires tells us something too. Ted's in contact with the police and they're working together to narrow the possibilities down, find who's doing this before

he does any more harm or gets someone killed.'
He shrugged. 'It's not easy, but it's all he can do.'

'You think it's a man. The fire-raiser.'

'Statistically that's the probability. This kind
of fire isn't usually a woman's weapon.' He
shrugged. 'But you can't rule anything out. In
the end it's all just probabilities.'

He was staring at nothing. Going through those
probabilities in his mind, trying to make some
sense of them. Almost as far away as when he'd
been with Ted for the afternoon.

'Eat. It'll get cold.' She picked up her own fork
and speared a chip from his plate.

'Hey, you've got your own.'

'Yeah, but stolen chips always taste better.'

They ate in silence. Abby was hungry, and Nick
had obviously worked up an appetite that afternoon as well. And even though it was still early,
the hours of darkness were already beckoning
her. What would he do? Would he find her again?
Ask her up to his room? Every time she thought
about it Abby felt a tightening in her chest, a sudden thump of her heart against her ribcage.

The waitress had brought coffee and Abby had

just taken her first sip when Pete arrived, sitting down at their table without his usual *'Can I join you?'* That, and the look on his face already had Nick's full attention.

'What is it, mate?'

Pete turned to Abby. 'Could you come and take a look at Louise? She's not well.'

Abby took another sip of her coffee. 'Of course, I'll come straight up as soon as I've finished. What's the problem?'

Pete and Nick exchanged glances and Nick stood. 'We need to go now, Abby.'

Nick was right in not allowing any delay. 'I noticed that she wasn't at dinner and went to find her,' Pete explained briefly on the stairs. 'I don't like the look of her. One of the guys said that he thought she'd cut her foot but he wasn't sure whether it was when she was in the water.'

'Okay. Let me see. Maybe she's got a bug of some sort, in which case a couple of paracetamol and a good night's sleep will do the trick.' Abby hoped so. Louise hadn't said anything about a cut, and cuts sustained in the open water could go septic with frightening speed.

Pete opened the door to Louise's room without knocking and ushered Abby inside. Louise was curled up on the bed, wrapped tightly in the thick bedspread, even though the evening wasn't cold.

'Hey, Louise. I hear you're not feeling too well.' Abby sat down on the bed beside her.

'I'm okay. Go away, Abby, I just need to rest up for tomorrow.' Louise didn't even open her eyes.

She most definitely wasn't okay, but Abby wasn't about to start a wrestling match to get the bedspread away from her. 'Have you cut your foot? May I have a look at it?'

'It's okay, Abby. Leave me alone.' Louise's voice was half a plea, half a rejection.

'Come along, now, Louise.' Nick's voice was gentle but unmistakeably an order. Abby scooted along to the end of the bed as he took her place, sitting next to Louise, lifting her slightly and pulling the bedspread away from her. Almost unconsciously, Louise obeyed.

'That's it.' Nick had her cradled against his chest. 'Now, tell me where you cut yourself.'

'In the water, boss.' Louise allowed him a smile and relaxed against him.

Nick shook his head, but now wasn't the time for recriminations. 'When?'

'The day before yesterday. When we went for a practice swim.'

'Okay, well, Abby needs to look at it. Just hold still a minute.'

Louise did what she was told, extending her left leg towards Abby. A loose sock covered her foot, and as Abby stripped it off, Louise winced.

'Okay. Let's see now.' Abby really didn't need to see any more. Louise had dressed the cut with lint and plasters, but the leg was badly swollen and bright, livid red. 'I'm going to take the dressing off now.'

Nick's arms closed around Louise, holding her tightly, and she cried out as Abby pulled the plaster off. The cut was barely more than an inch long, hidden behind her ankle, but it was deep and seeping blood and pus. Nick's jaw hardened when he saw it.

Well, it might. The cut was obviously infected, and Louise's drowsy, disoriented state indicated that some of the infection was already in her bloodstream, working its way around to her heart, her lungs, her kidneys.

'Pete, can you get the car and bring it round to the front door? Nick, wrap her up in the bed-spread. Leave her leg free.'

'Isn't there anything you can do here?' Pete asked her quietly.

'What she really needs is high-strength anti-biotics. The only place we can get those is the hospital. We need to go now.'

'Okay. I'll send one of the lads up to carry her down.'

Abby nodded to Pete and went into the en suite bathroom to wash her hands. Then back to Louise's side. She put her hand on her forehead. 'Not too much of a temperature. And her pulse is steady.' She gave an exclamation of frustration. 'I wish I had my medical kit here.'

'It's you she needs. Will it do any good to clean the wound?' Nick's voice was quiet, steady, and Abby's heartbeat racheted down a notch.

'We'll just be wasting time. It's not the wound itself I'm worried about, it's the poison in her bloodstream. The only way to deal with that is to get her to the hospital.'

Sam came bursting through the door at a run and Nick hoisted Louise up into his arms, passing her to Sam. Quickly the small group negotiated the stairs, and Nick and Sam put Louise into the back of the waiting car.

'Abby, you go in the back with her.' He looked at Pete. 'Okay if I take her?'

'Can you manage?'

'It's an automatic. And Louise is still part of my crew.'

Pete nodded imperceptibly and threw Nick the car keys. He slid into the driver's seat, programming the satnav, and took a look over his shoulder to make sure that Louise and Abby were settled. Then he jammed the gear lever into drive and put his foot down.

Nick had drawn up outside the A and E department of the hospital, and Abby had gone to get a wheelchair, taking Louise inside while Nick parked the car. By the time he got back, Abby was talking intently to the receptionist.

She seemed to be pressing her point, producing her own hospital ID from her purse, and the receptionist called a nurse. The nurse took one look at Louise's foot and called a doctor, and Louise was pushed quickly through the doors into the treatment area with Abby in tow, leaving Nick to sit and contemplate the wall.

He hated this. Always, whenever a member of his crew was hurt, he'd make it to the hospital as soon as humanly possible. And always he'd get stuck in some waiting room, the last to hear what was happening and unable to help or influence what was going on behind closed doors.

The doors to the treatment area shook, and caught Nick's eye. Then they opened, and Abby's head appeared, closely followed by her beckoning hand.

'What? What is it?' He made it to his feet and over to her in double-quick time.

'Nothing. It's okay. I just thought you'd like to come in and see her.'

Warmth fizzed and flickered across his chest. 'Yeah. I would. Thanks.'

She opened the doors, letting him through, and

led him along the row of treatment bays, stopping outside one at the far end. 'I've spoken to the doctor who's treating her and everything's fine. I have no cause for concern.'

'What's the matter with her, Abby?' Nick matched her low tone, careful that they could not be overheard from inside the cubicle.

'Well, that cut's obviously infected, and the blood test indicates she has a mild case of septicaemia.' She laid her hand on his chest in response to his start. 'But we caught it early. She's had a blood test and they're checking her vital organs to make sure the infection hasn't reached them, but she seems fine. You'll see a big difference in her once the antibiotics have kicked in.'

'Will they keep her here?'

'Overnight certainly. They'll probably let her go some time tomorrow or the next day, once she's seen a specialist and all the test results are through. In the meantime, they'll be putting her on a drip to get the antibiotics into her system as quickly as possible. She's getting saline as well, she's been sick and she's pretty dehydrated.'

'Good. Thanks, Abby. I wish Louise had said something about it.'

'One of the symptoms of septicaemia can be impaired judgement. People can just wander off on their own or curl up in a corner, as Louise did.'

'I should have seen that she had a cut when she went into the water yesterday. I should have checked.' Nick wanted to punch the wall but he had to make do with mentally kicking himself. The harder the better.

'It was easy to miss. I did when I helped her on with her wetsuit. Everyone knows about cuts, you've said it often enough.'

'Obviously not loudly enough.'

'If you'd said it any louder, my ears would have started to bleed. Let it go, Nick.' She gave him a little smile and turned to lead him into Louise's cubicle.

Louise looked better. Even though the saline and antibiotic drips had only just been set up and couldn't be taking effect yet, she seemed much more cheerful. Much more together. She was biting her lip as Nick squeezed himself into a corner by her bedside, out of the way of the technician who was removing the last of the heart monitor's sticky pads from her arm.

'Sorry, Nick.'

He grinned. 'You'd better be. I'm getting too old for this. Let me digest my dinner next time before you scare me out of my wits, eh?'

A tear escaped Louise's eye and Nick took the tissue that Abby had produced out of nowhere and gave it to her. 'I should have done something about the cut straight away. But it was so small, and it seemed okay. I wanted to swim and go to the fair and I thought it would be all right.'

'Forget it. These things happen.'

'I made a mistake.' Louise seemed intent on giving herself a hard time.

'We all make mistakes. I've made a few that would make your hair stand on end.' Not Abby's. He'd told her everything and she'd hardly blinked. Had slept next to him afterwards, as well, sprawled across his chest as if he somehow had a right to be close to her.

'Really?' Louise's voice bumped him back down to earth. Appealing to her curiosity had obviously done what reassurance couldn't and she was smiling now.

'Yeah, really. One of these days maybe I'll tell you about them.' Nick manoeuvred himself into the plastic chair by the side of the bed, awkward in the tight space. 'In the meantime, your job is to get better. Is there anything you need me to do?'

'Will you call my mum and dad?'

'Of course. I'll tell them that you're on the mend, eh?'

'Yes…yes, do that.' Louise shot Abby a querying look.

'You'll be feeling much better soon. Well enough to tell them yourself.' Abby gave her an encouraging smile. 'We'll call them tonight, and let them know that you're safe and sound, and that you'll speak to them in the morning. I'll ask Pete to arrange for someone to come in and bring you a phone.'

Louise nodded. 'Thanks. You've got their number.' She turned to Nick. 'It's on the sheet I filled out.'

'I've got it.' He leaned forward, taking Louise's

hand in his. 'Just concentrate on getting better, okay? Leave everything else to me.'

'Okay. Thanks, Nick.' She let out a sigh. 'I won't be able to swim tomorrow, then.'

'No, you won't.' Abby's voice was firm.

A little thrill worked through Nick's system. 'Don't worry about that. We'll get someone to swim in your place.' He didn't meet Abby's eye. Tomorrow's swim was the second short swim, only two miles. Everyone was already taking part. Everyone but him.

Louise grimaced. 'There is no one else, Nick. You know that.' She giggled suddenly. 'Unless you can fit Pete's belly into a wetsuit.'

'Nah. We don't want to frighten anyone.' Nick shrugged. 'I may do it myself.'

He could feel the force of Abby's disapproval burning into the back of his neck, but she said nothing. Nick imagined that she was waiting until they were out of Louise's earshot to make her views plain, and the thought of being on the end of her passion sent a shiver of expectation through his stomach.

'You can't…can you?' Louise looked unconvinced.

'We'll see, eh? Just let me sort that one out.'

'Okay, boss.' Louise relaxed against the pillows, looking up at the bags of saline and antibiotics above her head. 'It's not dripping very fast. Is that right?'

Nick chanced a look at Abby, who had focussed on the valve at the bottom of the bag of antibiotics, tapping it gently. 'It's okay. Little bit sluggish, maybe. Try clenching your hand and releasing it…like this.'

Louise obeyed and the drip responded, speeding up slightly.

'Yeah, that's right.' She flipped a glance at Nick. 'Give her your hand, Nick. Squeeze on his fingers, Louise. As hard as you like. That's it. Don't worry about hurting him.'

So that was how it was, was it? He was in for an ear-bashing later on, that was plain. Nick chuckled softly.

CHAPTER TEN

'So who do you have in mind for tomorrow? To swim?' They were walking across to the car park in the gathering dusk, having made sure that Louise was settled comfortably for the night. Abby decided to broach the subject gently. It was just possible that Nick had someone other than himself in mind to substitute for Louise.

He was grinning. Dammit, she'd known all along what he intended to do. 'I was thinking of doing it myself.'

Abby swallowed her concern for him, which was quickly turning to rage. 'Do you think that's a good idea?'

'I think I'm the only one who can do it.' He was still grinning.

'Nick.' Stay calm. Don't rise to the bait. 'You're recovering from a fractured patella and a torn cartilage. I know it feels better now, but you still need to take things carefully.'

'I've been doing a bit of swimming, and my leg's been fine. Dr Patel told me that it was good exercise, as long as I didn't push it.'

That's right. Throw her boss's words at her. 'And you reckon that a two-mile, open-water swim isn't pushing it, do you?'

'I'll stop if I get into difficulties. I have a neoprene support that I wear in the water.'

'Right. Pull the other one. If you get into the water, you'll be damned rather than get out anywhere other than the finishing point.'

He shrugged. 'Dr Patel—'

'Doesn't know you the way I do.'

He chuckled. 'No. I'll give you that.'

'Oh-h!' Abby threw up her arms in frustration. 'Don't play that card with me, Nick. My concerns are strictly professional.'

'Aw. Don't you care? Just a little bit?' He advanced towards her, eyes as dark as melted chocolate, and Abby felt her resolve beginning to waver.

'Don't you dare, Nick Hunter.'

'Dare what, Abby? Dare to touch you?'

'Don't you dare try to control me.'

'Oh, so this is about control now, is it? I thought you were worried about my knee.'

'I am.' Abby was near tears. Why couldn't he see? He was trying to make everything right and the thought that he might hurt himself in the process was too much to bear. 'But it's all the same thing, Nick. You can't make a thing happen just because you will it to. If you're not fit to swim then you're not fit, and no amount of wishful thinking on your part is going to change that.'

'I'm okay. Like I said, I won't push it. If I feel that I'm doing my knee any damage, I'll stop.'

'And like I said. I don't believe you. You'll just keep going, whatever.'

'Well, we're just going to have to agree to disagree on that one.' Nick pulled the car keys out of his pocket and thumbed the key fob to disengage the locks. 'Get into the car.'

'I'll drive.'

'Oh, and I can't drive a car now. Anything else you want to put on the list of things I'm not allowed to do on medical grounds?'

'I said I'll drive. Either that or I take the bus home.' She could at least be in charge of her own destiny, even if she couldn't persuade Nick to do what she wanted.

'Fine.' He dropped the keys into her hand. 'Have it your way. Do you even know the way back to the hotel?'

He got into the passenger seat of the car and reached for the satnav. 'Leave it, Nick. That's another thing I can manage to do without your help.'

They drove in silence. Abby concentrated on the road ahead, rather than think about Nick. How infuriating he was. How it made her heart hurt when she thought about how hard he drove himself. She slid the car into one of the parking spaces in the hotel car park and got out, waiting for him to slam the passenger door before she engaged the central locking.

'Wait.' She had stalked into the hotel ahead of him, but he caught her arm before she could make it across the reception area and to the stairs.

'What is it, Nick? You don't see things my way, and I'm not going to argue with you any more.'

They'd argued before, more times than she cared to count. But this time it had gone too far, and the corrosive silence in the car had finished the job that words had started, building an impenetrable barrier between them. His face was closed, impassive. Still unbearably handsome, and it almost killed her to pull her arm from his grasp and run up the stairs.

Okay, so I'm concerned for him. So shoot me. Someone was going to have to. Serious injury or death were about the only things right now that were going to get Nick Hunter out of her system.

Day Three. Buttermere. Two miles.

The day was idyllic, sunlight caressing the mountains and trees around the lake and shimmering across the crystal-clear water. Today had been designed as a treat for the swimmers, a manageable distance in a quiet, clean lake surrounded by spectacular scenery.

Nick slid into the water and began to swim gently up and down along the shoreline to warm up. That morning he had seen what he'd refused to acknowledge last night. That Abby's resolutely closed door and the empty space in his bed, which still bore a trace of her scent if he buried his face into her pillow, was all his fault.

He swam over to one of the escort boats, bobbing up and down in the water a few yards away. 'Pete. I thought you'd still be at the hospital.'

'They only let me stay half an hour, so I came straight back here.'

'How is Louise?'

'Fine. Looks a lot better than she did last night. She's spoken to her parents and she's got a bit of colour in her cheeks. Got stuck into the fruit that Abby sent, so she's got an appetite.'

'Abby sent fruit?'

Pete rolled his eyes. 'What, are you two not talking now? Louise liked your flowers as well, and I've got some change for you.'

'Any news about when she'll be out?'

'Today or tomorrow. The doctor hadn't seen her yet when I was there.'

'That's great, we can go and see her after lunch.'

'That's okay. Sam's going and I think he's taking one of the others with him. They don't like more than two visitors at once, and she needs a bit of peace and quiet, not a whole gang of us around her bed.' Pete's voice was firm. 'So what's this strategy you've got that doesn't involve using your leg, then?'

'Same one I was practising in the pool with the physio before we came here. I'm still using the leg, just not putting so much pressure on it. I could do to a mile and a half without any difficulties a week ago, so two shouldn't be a problem now.' He could have mentioned that to Abby last night, but he hadn't. Instead of reassuring her, he'd chosen to goad her, pretty much daring her to walk away from him, and it was a credit to her good sense that she had.

'Is Abby in on this?'

'No.'

Pete chuckled. 'So you're reckoning on surprising her with your ability to improvise, are you?'

There might have been something of that to it. Nick wasn't sure. 'Wait and see, mate.'

'I'll look forward to it. Just remember it's that way.' Pete pointed towards the finishing point on the other side of the lake. 'If you start swimming around in circles, I'm not going to fish you out.'

'Yeah. And if the boat sinks because you had too much breakfast, you're on your own, too.'

Pete waved him away, laughing, and Nick turned and swam back to the starting line, hanging onto the rope that was stretched between two buoys. Abby was some way away, her eyes fixed on the far shore of the lake, her head never once turning in his direction. Nick cursed himself again and waited for the siren to mark the start of the swim.

The siren sounded, and Nick struck out, keeping a little behind the other swimmers. His leg was stiff, but that was just the neoprene knee support over his wetsuit. His stroke didn't have its usual power, but it wasn't bad. The test had begun. Whether he could do this swim. Whether he would give up if he couldn't. If giving up was what it took, he'd do it, for Abby's sake if not his own.

His confidence was growing, and he fell into a rhythm. Slowly he began to draw ahead of the other swimmers, striking out with more assurance as he found that he could do so without pain.

Caught up in the exhilaration of being back in the water, feeling the muscles of his shoulders stretch and bunch as he sliced through the calm, shimmering surface, he didn't notice that someone else was with him until he got almost to the centre of the lake. Nick took the luxury of a look behind him and saw that he was ahead of the pack. All but one of them.

He could see Abby's bright swim cap bobbing in the water just behind and to the left of him. He stopped, treading water, to give her time to catch up with him.

For a moment he thought she was going to swim straight past him, but with an abrupt splash she veered towards him, ending up treading water opposite him.

'Interesting style you have there. How's it going?'

'Good. Swim with me?'

She didn't answer but started to swim, a mid-paced crawl, which kept them ahead of the pack but didn't stretch either of them. Nice and easy.

Just get to the finishing post. Nick adjusted his rhythm to hers, a hundred strokes. Two hundred. Three.

She had a sweet style. It was like everything she did, precise, graceful and yet with a hint of audacity. The feeling that at any moment she might break out of her rhythm, toss her head and do something wild and beautiful. The way she had when she'd made love with him. Nick took another hundred strokes to ponder that, finding that it wasn't nearly enough and that he was still thinking about it as they neared the finishing buoy.

He picked up the pace slightly, and she matched him. A little more, and she was still with him, her body sliding through the water. The urge to push her even further, see what they could do together, was growing.

Against all reason, Nick struck out as strongly as he could. It wasn't too far now, just a few hundred yards. She responded to his silent challenge, kicking out, her legs pushing her forward in the water.

They were almost equally matched. Nick's

arms and shoulders were much more powerful than hers, but he was hampered by the brace on his leg and by the fact that he couldn't kick as strongly. Resisting the temptation to change back to his usual style and use his legs more, he put all of his effort into his shoulders and arms.

She was slicing through the water. He fell behind slightly and she made the most of her advantage, swimming as if there were sharks in the water behind her. Nick put his head down and concentrated hard on the finishing buoy, the raw excitement of the chase flooding his system. This had been brewing for a while now, and it felt good to get the corrosive energy of all the things left unsaid between them out of his system. From Abby's determined stroke, it looked as if she felt exactly the same.

His fingers touched the buoy and he almost crashed into it. He had no idea of whether he'd beaten her or not, until he felt her hand grab his arm and she touched home. She was breathing heavily, her eyes shining with the same thrill that he felt. Planting her hands on his shoulders, she used the weight of her body as she levered it up-wards to duck his head beneath the water.

He broke the surface, laughing and shaking the water from his hair. 'What's that for?'

'Not telling me that you've invented a new stroke. What do you call it, the Crabby Fireman?'

'Suppose I deserve that.'

'You do.'

It was an unashamed come-on and Nick was nothing if not equal to a challenge. He kissed her, full on the lips, pressing his claim on her until surprise turned to passion and she wrapped her legs around his waist. It was only when he felt the wake of the boat hit them that he released her, turning to wave, while she sheltered behind his bulk.

'So who won?' Pete was up on the deck, grin-ning down at them.

It wasn't a straightforward question. 'I made the buoy first.' He felt her leg wind around his in the water. 'Abby won on style, though.'

In the activity surrounding the end of the swim and then lunch at the hotel, Abby had seemed to lose touch with Nick again. He was there, beside her, but there were too many people around. What she wanted to say to him didn't need an audience.

Everyone had dispersed, to their rooms or onto the patio to talk lazily in the sun. And Abby was on a mission. She tapped gently on Nick's door, knowing that he was in there.

'Hey.' His smile, and the way he stepped back from the door immediately, gave her confidence.

'I just came to collect my other swimsuit. I left it in your bathroom.'

'I was going to bring it to you. If you hadn't come.'

'Thanks.' Abby swallowed hard and made for the bathroom. If she was just here for the swimsuit, why had she bothered to go up to her room before lunch and change into the soft leather boots and the gypsy skirt she liked so much?

Her swimsuit was folded neatly on the vanity unit. She picked it up, catching sight of herself in the mirror and stopping to adjust a stray lock of hair.

'You look nice. Lovely, in fact.'

'Oh? Do I?' Abby tried to make out that she

was surprised by the comment. 'It's just an old skirt.'

'Going anywhere?'

She shook her head. 'No, I've nothing planned for this afternoon.' She may as well get it over with. 'I didn't give you a chance to explain last night. I should have trusted you.'

'I don't see why. It's not as if I'm a stranger to unrealistic expectations. I should have told you.' He sat down on the bed. 'I owe you an apology, Abby.'

'I think that's my line.'

'What, you owe yourself an apology? What for?' The deliberate misinterpretation and his wayward grin told her that nothing more was needed. They both knew what they'd done and now it was behind them.

'Does this mean I'm redundant now?'

'What?' His surprise was genuine. 'No, Abby. Why, did you think I was going to try and take over from you?'

'The thought crossed my mind. You took all the precautions and you're fit to swim.' She wouldn't have blamed anyone in Nick's place for taking over the final swims, just out of spite. But spite wasn't really Nick's style.

He shook his head. 'I was fit to swim two miles. On one day. I'd be asking for trouble if I tried to do any more. Anyway, this is your project now. Don't you want to finish it?'

Abby breathed a sigh of relief. 'Of course I do. I just thought…'

'I wouldn't take the swim over from you, even if I was fit. It wouldn't be fair on either of us. I'm happy to have done as much as I could and now I'm going to quit.' He stood, taking a couple of steps towards her. 'Come here.'

There was nothing more to say. She closed the gap between them, letting him take her in his arms. Losing herself in the hunger of his kiss, the sweetness of his desire. Somehow managing to twist the buttons of his shirt open so that when she ran her hands across his shoulders there was nothing to stop her from feeling the smooth ripple beneath his skin.

'Stay with me this afternoon, Abby.'

'Yes.'

He kissed her again, moulding her body against

his. 'Got to warn you. If you don't take your clothes off in the next ten seconds, I'm going to do it for you.'

The raw power of his frame, the strength of his desire only lent a greater edge to his tenderness. Her allotted ten seconds were just enough to slip her boots off, and then he took over, undoing a couple of buttons on her blouse before losing patience and pulling it over her head.

Scattering their clothes on the floor, drinking in her kisses like a man possessed, he backed her towards the solid, old-fashioned sideboard, reaching for the condoms on the way. There was barely time for him to catch up a pillow from the bed to cushion her from the wooden surface, before he lifted her up, perching her in front of him.

'Abby...' His voice was deep, urgent.

'I know. I know. Me too.' She wrapped her legs around his waist, leaning back, her arms supporting her. There was no possibility of prolonging the moment this time. It had to be now.

'Look at me.' His words cut through the haze of wanting. 'Look at me, Abby.' She looked at him. Stared into his eyes as he slid inside her, watching the pupils dilate even further, every movement of their bodies reflected in his face.

She was gasping for breath, almost whimpering with pleasure. She was caught in his gaze, knew that he must be able to see everything she was feeling, and she didn't care. Nick dominated her completely, and she had never felt so free. Nothing had ever felt this right.

One hand left her leg, and brushed against her breast, sending new jolts of sensation through her. Swiftly, tenderly, mercilessly he took her to the very edge, keeping her there for agonised moments until she felt her body respond to his caress once more, shaking uncontrollably as he moved inside her, drawing out her pleasure until there was nothing more to feel.

The balance tipped. As her own body began to relax, his tightened. He coiled one arm around her, supporting her back, planting his other hand behind her on the sideboard.

'Abby. Please…' He was trembling now, pressing her to his chest.

'It's okay, Nick.' She soothed him gently. Here in the sunlight, face to face and unable to hide anything from each other, the intimacy would have been terrifying if she didn't want it so much. Tightening her legs around his waist, she rolled her hips and he roared out his release.

For long moments neither of them moved, still shaken by the enormity of what had happened between them. Then he kissed her, his lips tender on hers.

'Come to bed, Nick.'

He wrapped his arms around her, hugging her tight, seemingly unwilling to move. 'I'm not so sure I can walk just yet.'

She giggled, straightening up and clasping her hands behind his neck. 'I'll throw you over my shoulder, then.' She almost felt that she could. She felt she could do anything right now.

'Oh, yeah? Like to see you try it.'

CHAPTER ELEVEN

NICK groaned as he pulled himself back from the velvet darkness of sleep. Abby was lying on her back next to him, her head propped up on his chest, her fingers locked with his. All he could feel was pure, sated happiness.

'You awake, sweetheart?' He knew she was. Even though he couldn't see her face, he could see her eyelashes, fluttering gently against the profile of her cheek.

'Yes.'

That was all that needed to be said. For the next few minutes anyway. She'd done it again. Ripped him apart, claimed each piece of him for her own and then effortlessly put him back together again. Nick wondered if her name was now stamped right through him, like on a stick of rock.

'What's the time?'

He looked at his watch. 'Half-past six. Plenty of time before dinner.'

'Good.' She shifted, rolling over onto her side and tucked her shoulder under his arm, snuggling in close. 'I'm too comfortable to move.'

'Me too.' Nick allowed himself to run his fingers across her shoulder. The softest, most velvet skin on her body. Or perhaps that was her belly. Or her breasts. He'd have to run through the options again before he made a decision.

'We could always miss dinner. Get something sent up.'

'Oh, no.' He twisted his head around so he could catch her eye. 'You need to keep your calorie intake up. No skipping meals.'

'Right.' She gave a mock salute. 'Boss.'

Nick felt the chuckle, coming up from somewhere deep inside his soul and rumbling through his chest. 'So long as you know it.' She aimed a play punch at his shoulder and he twisted away, wincing as he felt the muscles pull. 'Steady on with the shoulder. It's already taken a bit of a beating today.'

'You should have said. I could have massaged it for you.'

'I think you did, didn't you?' After that first, earth-shattering embrace, they'd taken their time. Spent hours, touching, massaging, learning each other's bodies. A long, slow burn when Abby had finally let go of the last vestiges of her self-sufficiency and laid claim on her pleasure. Their pleasure. She'd driven him half-mad from sheer sensual overload by the time she'd finished with him.

'That was different. Therapeutic massage can hurt a little when you ease the knots out.'

'Definitely not therapeutic, then. I was hurting much more than a little.'

She chuckled. 'That was your own fault. I seem to remember you were the one calling the shots at that point.'

'I loved every minute of it.' Every second. Every move she made and each one of her soft sighs. Nick wondered whether he should tell her that and decided against it. They sounded too much like the words of a man who was falling in love.

'Me too.' She rolled away from him, stretching luxuriantly.

'I was thinking of driving over to see Ted Bishop tomorrow afternoon.'

'Again?' She grinned at him. 'I thought you weren't involved with the case any more. That you'd done your bit and you were on holiday now.'

'That's absolutely true. I could give you the excuse that Ted's a friend. I don't get to see him much when I'm down in London.'

'You could. I'll reserve the right to take that with a handful of salt. Any wounds anywhere I could rub it into?'

'All over the place. I can't guarantee that the conversation won't touch on the arson case. But if you're not too tired after the swimming, would you like to come with me?'

'So you're not going to sneak off this time without telling anyone.'

'Not without telling you.'

'Do I get to see a fire engine up close?'

'Yeah, if you want to. I can call him and we'll meet up at one of the fire stations. The guys there will undoubtedly tell you more than you ever wanted to know about a fire engine if you express even the mildest interest.'

She chuckled. 'In that case, you've definitely got a date.'

Day Four. Derwent Water. Four miles.

Four miles, and Nick was with her all the way. The stiff breeze, which whipped the water into white peaks, was not enough to stop Abby from making the distance within the planned time, and the group arrived back at the hotel to find that Louise was back and confined to her room.

'Thought you were going to have lunch upstairs with Louise?' Nick grinned at her as Abby sat down opposite him in the dining room.

'I was, but she got a better offer. Sam's up there with her.'

'Really?'

'Yes. Keep it quiet.'

'Why?' Nick looked puzzled.

Abby rolled her eyes. 'I thought you didn't miss anything. Louise thinks that Sam's really cute.'

'Sam? Cute?' The combination of the two words had obviously not occurred to Nick before. 'I've heard him called a few things, but cute's never been one of them. What have they been giving her in that hospital?'

'Don't be like that. Sam's really sweet. And he's obviously got a soft spot for Louise as well.'

Nick shrugged. 'Well you're obviously privy to some insider information here so I'll take your word for it.' He leaned across the table towards her, his words almost drowned in the hubbub of conversation around them. 'So what about me, then? Am I cute?'

'Not a chance.' Abby laughed at Nick's injured expression. 'You're *very cute.*'

He made a gesture of mock horror, but the grin didn't leave his face for the duration of the meal and he was still smiling when he collected Pete's car keys from him and ushered her out of the hotel.

'You look nice.' His hand strayed to the small of her back and stayed there and he leaned close as they walked. 'Extremely cute.'

'Thank you.' Abby felt her cheeks flush. She'd hoped that the time she'd taken with her appearance this afternoon wouldn't show.

'Sweet as well. You always look sweet.' His thumb moved against her spine. 'I like your hair loose. And that reddish colour suits you.'

'It's raspberry.' She reckoned her face was about the same shade as her woollen jacket at the moment.

'Hmm.' He took advantage of the fact that the car park was screened from view from the hotel by a stand of trees and twisted her round against the car, pressing his lips against hers. 'Not strawberry?'

'I don't think so.' She pulled him against her.

'Maybe I should make completely sure.' He kissed her again. Tender enough to melt her heart. Demanding enough to set it clamouring for more.

'Ow. What's that?' Something was digging into her ribs and Abby slid her fingers inside his fleece jacket and pulled a rolled-up newspaper from the deep inside pocket.

He chuckled quietly. 'Local newspaper. Mrs Pearce says that there's an article about us on page four.'

'Oh, well, let's have a look, then.' Abby unrolled the newspaper and spread it out on the roof of the car, turning the pages. 'Here it is.' She scanned the article carefully.

Nick was reading too, over her shoulder. Suddenly, abruptly, she felt him tense and then turn away.

'What? What's the matter, Nick?'

He wasn't looking at her. He didn't seem to be looking at anything in particular, just a point in the middle distance that didn't exist. Abby turned back to the newspaper, scanning the pages, and then she saw it. It took a moment for the words to sink in, and she reread them with growing horror as it became plain that her eyes were not deceiving her.

'What on earth….? Who wrote this? It's all lies!'

'No, Abby, it's not.' He leaned against the car next to her. 'There has been a spate of arson attacks in this area. I'm consulting with the local fire authorities. And I am an ex-junkie.' His eyes were dull. Dead.

She wanted to shake him. Or kick him. Anything to make him fight. 'It's not true, Nick. They're making it sound as if drug taking is the only thing you've ever done. Here…' she stabbed at the paper with her finger '…it says *"a drug user, currently suspended from active duty"*.'

'I am.'

'You're someone who had a problem with drugs, overcame it years ago, and is now off sick with an unrelated injury, sustained in the course of duty. That's entirely different.' Abby grabbed his arm, digging her fingers into his biceps. 'Nick, stop this.'

'Yeah.' His grin barely made it to the sides of his lips, let alone up to his eyes. 'Nothing I can do about it. Best thing to do is just ignore it and get on with the job in hand.'

'Yes. Unless I see that creep of a reporter again.' Abby had noticed the name at the head of the article. 'How did this Graham Edson guy get all of this? We hardly spoke to him.'

Nick shrugged. 'Maybe Ted wanted to give me some good press and mentioned my name. Maybe Edson recognised my key fob when he picked my keys up and put two and two together. Rings up HR, gets chatting to someone and then slips in how good it is that I've been clean for a while. All it takes is for someone to agree, in all innocence, and he's got his confirmation.'

Abby felt sick. It was that easy to take a man's career and trash it in the papers. At least this was just a local paper. She swept the newspaper off the roof of the car, screwing it up into a tight ball, and stalked over to the wastepaper bin. She would have completed the gesture and set fire to it, only she knew that Nick's first instinct would be to put it out again.

He was still leaning against the car, watching her quietly. She couldn't bear this. The way he accepted it as if it was his due. Grabbing the front of his jacket, she pulled him close. 'We can deal with this.'

'Yeah.' His eyes had softened, but he kept his hands in his pockets. 'Look, what do you say we give this afternoon a miss?'

'Why? What else do you want to do?'

'I'll go and see Ted. I was just thinking that it would be better if you stayed here.'

She didn't need to ask. Abby knew exactly why Nick wanted her to stay behind. 'I don't think so.' If he thought that she was ashamed to be seen with him just because of a stupid newspaper article, he didn't know her very well.

'I may be taking a little flak because of this. Not from Ted, not from the guys here. But I don't want you to get mixed up with it, Abby.'

'You think I can't deal with whatever anyone dishes out?'

His shoulders relaxed a little. 'No. Will you be able to handle me not being able to deal with it?'

Abby grinned at him. 'Piece of cake. I can handle you any day of the week, Nick Hunter. Get into the car.'

Abby stuck to him like glue, sliding her fingers around the crook of his arm when they walked into the fire station together and practically needing to be prised away from him by the young firefighter who had volunteered to show her around while he talked business with Ted. Nick watched, a faint stab of resentment catching him as someone else's hands guided her up into the driver's seat of the fire truck, and then turned back to Ted.

'It's my fault. I should never have said any-thing about it.'

It was bad enough having to think about this latest humiliation, let alone talk about it, but Ted had obviously been beating himself up about it. 'I'm not in hiding, Ted, there's nothing wrong with mentioning my name. This might not be my choice, but it's not the end of the world. I always said that if it came out, it came out.'

Ted grunted, unconvinced. 'You never said anything of the sort.'

'If you say so. I always thought it, though.'

'Just thinking things doesn't get you anywhere.' Ted was looking at Abby, pointedly.

'Leave her out of it, Ted.'

'Is that what you're doing?'

'I'm trying.' Nick frowned. 'Without much suc-cess at the moment.'

Ted chuckled. 'That figures. Most women have a protective streak a mile wide.'

Abby wasn't most women. And Nick had been secretly loving the way she'd stuck by him so fiercely, like a mother bear with her cub. Ready to cuff him if he stepped out of line but reserving her full fury for anyone who dared to confront him. He didn't need her to defend him, but the idea that she wanted to gave him a reason to hold his head up and face the world.

'She doesn't need to protect me, Ted, and neither do you. I'm okay. I'm not in any trouble over this.'

'As long as you know where to come if you are.'

'Of course I do. Thanks, mate.'

He dragged his gaze from where Abby was inspecting the inside of the fire-engine cabin, questioning her guide closely on something. Even at this distance she seemed to shine. As if there was a light source behind her pale blue eyes that threw everything around her into shadow. Nick wondered how much he could do with his life, what things he could achieve, with her smile to guide him, and shelved the thought. It wasn't going to happen.

He turned, indicating the pile of papers under Ted's arm. They promised to be a great deal simpler to deal with. 'So. Are those just for show, or have you got something for me?'

CHAPTER TWELVE

Day Five. Ullswater. Two miles.

Two easy miles, in preparation for the big one tomorrow. Eleven swimmers set off and eleven made the finish, Abby way ahead of them as usual, and as usual was escorted home by Nick on the support boat.

He looked tired. Not surprising after last night. When they returned from the fire station his mood of smiling optimism had seemed to dissolve and he'd gone to his room, on the excuse that he had to do some work for Ted.

When she'd tapped on his door late in the evening, he'd received her with a smile and asked her to stay, but he'd sat up most of the night in a small pool of light in the corner of the room, his laptop open in front of him.

He disappeared again after lunch, leaving Abby to spend the afternoon with Louise, who slept most of the time. By dinnertime she was bored with her book and frustrated with Nick.

'You're back.' She hardly raised her eyes from the pages when he knocked on Louise's door and quietly entered the room.

'I haven't been anywhere. She's asleep?'

'Yes.' Was that all he could say? He hadn't left the hotel but he'd been somewhere all right. With his father, maybe, telling him yet again to get out of his life and stay out. The ghost of a man that Abby didn't even know hung in the air between them, clamouring to be heard in the silence. Nick's brow furrowed and he beckoned her out of the room.

'What's up? Is she okay?'

'Yes, she's fine. She's had a major infection, it's taken it out of her.'

'Yes. Of course.' He sighed, running his hand back through his hair. 'As long as that's all it is.'

Abby shot him a glare. 'This is not about Louise. I'm more concerned about you.'

'Me?' He started guiltily. That slide of his eyes to one side, the way he couldn't quite face her told Abby that he had some inkling of what she was getting at.

Grabbing his hand, she marched him along the corridor and down the stairs to his room, closing the door firmly behind them. 'Why do I always have to prise everything out of you, Nick? I know when something's going on because you disappear on me. Can't you just talk to me?'

'I've got nothing to say, Abby. If you have, you'd better say it.'

The atmosphere in the room began to sizzle, like a pan heated up to boiling point, the lid rattling ominously. It felt good. At least Abby knew that Nick was there, not far away, in some place of his own that she couldn't reach.

'Fair enough. Some idiot writes something in a newspaper about you and suddenly you're hiding yourself away up in your room, pretending to work. Not sleeping. What do you think's going to happen? Do you truly believe that anyone who knows you is going to care?'

'I'm not *pretending* to work. And, yes, since you ask, I wouldn't blame anyone for thinking it makes a difference. I do.'

'Right. I know you do. If you want to think less of yourself because of what your father did and because something you did bore some faint resemblance to that, that's your prerogative. But don't expect me or Sam or Pete to just fall into line and think the worst of you because that's not what friends do. Have a little respect for us.'

'That's not fair, Abby. I respect you. I respect Sam and Pete.' He turned away from her and started to pace. Not a good sign. Pacing generally didn't augur well for any kind of amicable ending. Abby felt her shoulders slump and pulled herself upright to disguise her misery.

'Fine way you have of showing it.' She threw the words at him with an effort. If he was going to turn away from her again, she may as well get what she wanted to say off her chest.

His dark eyes blazed with defiance. 'Dammit, Abby, you don't know…'

'Then tell me. Show me. Don't just hide behind the mistakes you've made. Have the guts to come out and make some more.' Her chin was tilted aggressively towards him, and he took a step closer to her.

He took hold of her shoulders and the hairs on the back of her neck suddenly stood to attention. 'So what do you suggest I do?'

'Go downstairs and talk to them, Nick. It won't be the first time you've gone into a tough situation, knowing that they have your back.'

'This is different.'

'It's not. Trust me, Nick, it's not different.'

He pulled her towards him, wrapping his arms around her shoulders. Abby could hear his heart pumping, feel the kiss that he dropped on the top of her head. 'I...I do trust you, Abby.' The admission was obviously a difficult one for him to make, but it was a good one to hear, and Abby snuggled in closer to him.

'Let's go downstairs, then.'

'No. Not yet.' His hand slid down her back, turning the last dregs of anger into desire. 'Once again, we have unfinished business.'

Plenty of it. The energy that had been buzzing between them was sparking, crackling, looking for some kind of outlet. She reached up, finding the spot at the corner of his jaw that always made him shiver. 'So finish it, then.'

Nick had been as good as his word. It hadn't been easy for him, but he'd spread the newspaper on the table, in the lounge, made his confession and let Pete and Sam question him. It had been okay. Difficult, but okay. Just as she'd known it would be. And from the way Nick had squeezed her hand when he'd thought no one had been looking, it seemed that it was a relief to him as well.

They both lay on their backs on Nick's bed, staring at the canopy over their heads, talking. Both were fully clothed, and Abby wondered whether getting undressed and seducing him again would quell her night-before nerves. She guessed so, but Nick was having none of it, adamant that she needed to get a good night's sleep before swimming in the morning.

'What's the time?'

'Ten-thirty. You sleepy?' Nick raised himself up on one elbow.

'Yes. Kind of.'

'You think you might sleep if we went to bed?'

'Probably not.' Abby stretched and yawned. 'Perhaps in a while.'

'Okay. Come here.' He rolled her over on her side and curled up behind her. That felt so good. Leaning against his body, completely safe. Totally secure. Abby began to drift.

Quite what it was that woke her up, Abby wasn't sure. Maybe the crash of breaking glass. Maybe Nick, on the alert and rolling off the bed, dragging her with him. Whatever it was, Abby's eyes were open and she was wide awake before a sheet of flame began to engulf the curtains.

She was running before she could even think, Nick behind her, pushing her forwards towards the door. As soon as he made the corridor, he slammed the door closed behind him.

'What was that?' She asked the question to thin air. Nick was already halfway down the hallway, punching the alarm point on the wall, and bells echoed through the building. Pulling one of the two fire extinguishers that were fixed to the wall by the fire doors that led to the stairs, he lifted the heavy cylinder effortlessly.

He was going to go back in there. Abby wanted to scream at him, stop him somehow, but she swallowed her words. *This is his job. He knows what he's doing.*

Sam appeared from a nearby door, fully dressed, and gravitated to Nick's side. 'What's going on?'

'Something just came through my window. Looks like a petrol bomb. Check all the rooms in case there's anything else and get everyone together in the downstairs hallway. Get a couple of men outside, checking the grounds, and you find Louise and make sure she gets downstairs safely.'

'Okay, boss.' Other members of the team were appearing in the hallway, some dressed and others hastily pulling on their clothes, having already gone to bed. Sam quickly deployed the men and made for the stairs in the direction of Louise's room.

Abby flattened herself against the wall, acrid smoke entering her lungs. This wasn't good. She should get out but she couldn't leave Nick. She couldn't help him but she wouldn't leave him.

'Downstairs, Abby. With the others.' It was a point-blank command. Nick beckoned to one of the men, and the two of them gingerly opened the door, Nick going in first with the fire extinguisher.

Abby got halfway down the hallway. Far enough to be out of the way but close enough that she'd be there for Nick if he needed her. He seemed to have everything under control, but this was a volatile situation. People got hurt in volatile situations.

Nick had said it was a petrol bomb. Was this the work of the fire-raiser? She supposed it must be. Why here, though? She tried to go through all of the possibilities in her head, but she couldn't think. All she needed to know, right now, was that the fire was out and Nick was safe.

It seemed like an age, but finally he reappeared, his face and arms streaked with smoke and sweat. 'Abby…' There was a warning note to his voice.

'I heard. Is it out?'

'Yeah. We need to keep an eye on it, in case it re-ignites, but we got to it quickly.' He shook his head slightly, as if he knew that he'd been diverted from his original purpose. 'What are you doing still here?'

'Looking out for you two.'

'I told you…'

'Yes I know what you told me.'

He rolled his eyes, but he was grinning. 'Fire is *my* job.'

'And potential casualties are mine.'

He shrugged, as if he knew that he wasn't going to get any further on this one. He was learning. 'Would you like to go downstairs and see if you can find any casualties down there, then? I'm afraid we're a bit short on any here.' He lifted his head as Sam hurried through the fire doors. 'Status?'

'There was another minor one in the dining room. All under control, no one hurt. We've called the police and the local fire service.' Sam grinned. 'Thought we'd better let them know we've been putting fires out on their patch.'

'Right. Where is everyone?'

'In the hallway. Louise is down there too.'

'Okay, we'll keep them there for the time being. It'll be easier to keep everyone safe if they're not wandering around outside. Everyone's got their eyes open?'

'Yep. I've got the guys checking outside and inside in twos.'

'Good. Nice job, Sam.'

Sam nodded. Nick's praise went unremarked on, but it was clearly not unheard. 'Do you think this is all there's going to be?'

'I don't know.' Nick was obviously worried. 'Will you stay here until you're sure that this one's safe? Got your phone?'

'Yes. Where's yours, though?'

Nick grinned. 'Let's see. It might be toast.'

Abby followed them into Nick's room. There were dark stains on the ceiling, the curtains were hanging in tatters, flapping in the breeze from the broken window. The smell of smoke and petrol. Abby didn't look at the black, charred section of carpet, just a few feet from the end of the bed, where whatever had been thrown through the window had rolled across the floor.

Nick picked up his phone from the bedside cabinet, checking it quickly. 'Looks okay.' A tone sounded from Sam's pocket. 'Yeah. Call me with anything.'

He caught Abby's hand and made for the door.

'We're off downstairs to find some casualties for the lady.'

'She can start with me. Louise bit me when I tried to carry her down the stairs. I might have blood poisoning.' Sam's voice floated after them.

'Serves you right,' Nick called back over his shoulder, without stopping.

CHAPTER THIRTEEN

HE HUSTLED her downstairs, where Pete was supervising while Mrs Pearce bellowed names from the hotel register, liberally dispensing her displeasure when people failed to answer promptly. Nick shot Pete a querying glance and Pete nodded. All okay down here.

Nick didn't let go of Abby's hand, and she followed him into the dining room. Partners, maybe? Or perhaps he just wanted to keep her close so he could keep an eye on her. He bent to inspect the charred carpet, wincing as he did so. In the heat of the moment Abby had forgotten all about his knee and Nick obviously had too.

'This one doesn't look as big as the other. Look.' He indicated the broken window. 'It came through there, but luckily the curtains were drawn back so they didn't catch. This is the seat of the fire, and it's definitely not as big as the one in my room.'

'So…' Abby couldn't see where he was going with this.

'So I reckon this one was the first. Then whoever it was moved past the front door, down that way.' He pointed towards the side of the building where his room was situated.

'What is this, Nick? Is it something to do with the arson cases that you're working on?'

'Looks like it. I imagine that he's been following his own press.'

Fear clutched at Abby's heart. 'You mean… he's after you?'

'I'm the one who got his name in the paper. And with all the publicity for the swimming, it wouldn't be too difficult to track me down.' His lips compressed into a thin line. 'I'm sorry, Abby, I've got you mixed up in this.'

'No, you haven't.' She dismissed the idea with a wave of her hand. 'So what do you think he's going to do next? Might he still be here?'

'That's my immediate concern. We need to know that everyone's safe and that there are no more petrol bombs about to come through any of the windows.' His face had a look of sheer, unstoppable determination. 'And catching him would be good.'

'Where do you think he might go next?'

'Probably kept going in the same direction then around the side of the building. There's plenty of cover around there from trees and bushes, and you can see what's happening at the front.' He seemed to come to some decision and he was on the move, halfway to the door. 'Come along.'

He led her upstairs and through the maze of corridors in the sprawling building, stopping opposite the door of Louise's room. 'We can see most of the side area from here.'

Flipping off the hall light, he took her hand and opened the door. Abby followed him into the darkened room, watching as he gingerly parted the curtains. 'Okay, stay low. Have a look around and see what you can see.'

She strained against the darkness outside, rough shapes emerging as her eyes began to acclimatise. 'Nick! Look, there's someone there.'

His hand was on her arm, steadying her. Or maybe stopping her from doing anything that he hadn't approved first. 'I see him.' Flame showed briefly behind a cupped hand, illuminating the face of a young man. Nick cursed quietly. 'The idiot's lighting a cigarette.'

Nick obviously wasn't worried about his lungs at the moment. Fire safety for arsonists. It would have been funny if the situation wasn't so serious.

Something flared and arced through the air. Nick almost threw her across the room towards the door, rugby-tackling her to the floor in the hallway. A whooshing sound reached her ears and she fought for breath.

'Get off me.' His weight was pinning her to the floor. Warm. Protective. And she couldn't breathe. He looked around quickly and then rolled away from her.

No flames or smoke. Nick was on his feet again, loping to the end of the hallway and opening the fire-escape door, and as she followed him Abby could see why. A petrol bomb had lodged in the branches of a tree, which was beginning to burn fiercely.

The sound of sirens came in the distance, suddenly swelling as flashing lights rounded the corner and a fire engine came to a stop outside, closely followed by a couple of police cars. Men were running towards the side of the building, and the dark shape below broke cover.

'Don't…' Nick roared into the darkness, and half slid, half ran down the fire-escape steps. His quarry had obviously decided that there was time for one last assault, and flame flared in his hand. This time, though, there was no up-lifted arm, swinging the deadly missile towards them.

Fire shot across the grass at his feet, and the figure jumped back and started to run. Flames were flickering around his arm, where he had spilled some of the petrol, and she heard Nick's cry of frustration as his leg finally gave way and he fell to the ground.

'Get down.' He was shouting now, scrambling towards the figure. 'Roll on the ground.'

The fleeing shape ignored him. Whether from panic, or pain, or determination not to be caught by the police, who were closing in fast, Abby couldn't tell. She ran down the fire-escape steps, following Nick across the uneven ground.

Their quarry took the low fence to the road in

one bound. Unable to slow his momentum, or maybe unable to see the danger, he threw himself right into the path of an oncoming car.

Nick let out a roar of agony. The young man's body catapulted upwards, as if suspended by invisible wires, which then snapped and dumped him back onto the roadway in a tangle of limbs.

He reached the motionless body a moment before one of the policemen, who stripped off his jacket and helped Nick douse what was left of the flames. By some instinct he seemed to know that Abby was right behind him, and he turned, yelling at the converging policemen, 'Let her through. She's a doctor.'

She knelt down in the middle of the road, police officers standing on both sides of her to stop any oncoming traffic. Somewhere in the back of her head, from the direction of the car, which had slewed wildly across the road, a woman's wails registered.

'We've got you, mate. Lie still and let the doctor look at you. Hang on.' Nick's voice. Trying to get through to a wounded man, give him some comfort.

She heard him call to a police officer to fetch a first-aid kit from one of the police cars. Unzipping the man's jacket, she quickly inspected the damage. The thick padding of his jacket had protected him from the fire, and his arm was pretty much untouched. It was the collision with the car that had done all the damage.

'What do you need, Abby?'

Her brain clicked into autopilot. 'Gloves...' She snapped on the surgical gloves and cleared the man's mouth. 'His breathing's shallow. Get someone to apply pressure to that leg to stop the bleeding.'

Nick passed another pair of gloves and padding from the first-aid kit to one of the policemen who had come shouldering his way through the group that had formed around them and reported as a first-aider.

She was dimly aware of the fact that Nick was holding the man's hand, and she could hear him talking to him. Trying to find a way to get through to him, tell him that someone was here for him and that he should live, not die here on the road.

'See if you can find a pulse.' Abby searched for some glimmer of hope and found it, beating threadily under her fingers and then slowing to a stop.

'CPR.' She braced herself over the man's chest and started to count. What she wouldn't do for a defibrillator right now. Adrenaline. Anything that might help save her patient. The sound of her own voice, counting, seemed unnaturally strident over the murmur of activity around them.

'Paramedic's here.'

'Right. Take over the chest compressions, will you, Nick, while we set up the defibrillator and the ventilation?'

She knew what needed to be done, but Abby also knew that she probably didn't have as much hands-on experience of this kind of thing as a paramedic. A man's life depended on her making the right decisions now.

'He's in asystole.'

Abby assessed the reading from the defibrillator carefully. It was her call, but she wanted the paramedic's view as well. 'I don't see any sign of VF.'

'Agreed.'

'He's not shockable, then. We'll give him adrenaline and continue CPR.'

They worked together for twenty minutes. Twenty minutes when there was little hope of even the slightest glimmer of life, but Abby wouldn't give up until they'd done everything according to the book. Finally she sat back on her heels.

It was her responsibility to declare the man dead, and she went through all the checks, waiting for the paramedic's agreement at each step. She took a deep breath. This was the first time she'd done this. 'I'm pronouncing him dead,' and followed it with the time.

She stripped off her surgical gloves, throwing them into the bucket that someone had provided for waste disposal. It seemed too heartless to just stand up and walk away, leave the man lying here on the road, the cannula and all the other paraphernalia that had been used to save him still in place. She knew they had to stay for the coroner's examination, but it seemed wrong somehow.

Nick laid the man's hand down on his chest,

and Abby realised that somehow he had managed to keep hold of it the whole time, without getting in the way of the work that she and the paramedic had been doing. At least there was that. Whenever the fragile spark of life had left that broken body, the man hadn't been completely alone.

Through the numbness she could feel Nick pulling her gently to her feet and guiding her away from the body. 'You're done here, Abby.'

She wouldn't cling to him now. Wouldn't cry either. She was surrounded by men who had seen this all before and she shouldn't let them know it was her first time. She'd seen death before, but she'd never been the one that everyone had looked to for those final words.

Nick did her the courtesy of not saying anything. There was nothing he could have said, he must know that. Just being here was good enough. The paramedic, on the other hand, seemed anxious to speak to her.

'Where are you from?'

'London. I work down in London.'

The man held out his hand. 'Steven Bell. Pleasure to meet you.'

Abby took his hand with trembling fingers, conscious that those few words were praise indeed from a man like this. The stoical, seen-it-all guys who spent their days on one of the sharpest ends of a tough profession. 'Thank you. Um… me too.'

She wasn't sure what she was meant to do next. Was she supposed to stay here? Sign something? Nick would know, he had to have seen this kind of thing before, but she didn't like to ask him in front of everyone. Abby was contemplating her next move when Nick made it for her, turning to Steven. 'The police will handle things from here on in?'

'Yes. I just need to get my paperwork straight and then I'll be off. This is my last call for this shift.'

Nick nodded. 'Cup of tea?'

'Yes. Thanks.'

She knew the exchange was all for her benefit, but she didn't care. Nick put his arm round Abby's shoulder and she followed his lead as he turned away from the little knot of people around the body.

* * *

It was two in the morning before Nick contrived to slip away with Abby to her room. He had insisted that she give her statement here and not at the police station, and tried to hurry things up, but there had beern procedures to go through. A man had died.

Abby had been keeping it all together, helping Mrs Pearce with tea and sandwiches for everyone, calmly recounting the events of the evening when questioned. She wasn't the sort to break down under pressure, and he respected her for it, but he hoped that now the pressure was off, she would start to let go.

She sat down on the bed, seeming weary suddenly, as if someone had tied lead weights to her limbs. Maybe she would talk about it now they were alone. Maybe not.

'Let's get you into the shower, eh?'

She sighed. 'You go first. I just want to sit here for a moment.'

He didn't want to leave her alone, but this wasn't about what he wanted—it was about what she needed. 'Okay. I'll be right here. Just call if you want me.'

'Yes. Thanks.'

When he emerged from the bathroom, pulling on a clean T-shirt that he'd borrowed from Sam, she was in exactly the same place that he had left her, still staring at her hands. He sat down beside her, careful not to touch her arm with his, and she hardly registered his presence.

'Some people…some people you just can't save. You know that as well as I do.'

'Yeah. I just feel so…' She shrugged. 'You know.'

'Yeah. I know.' That sickening feeling of loss, of helplessness, when things went horribly wrong and someone died. The first time was always the worst, but it didn't get much better after that. 'But you did everything that could have been done, Abby. Everything.'

'You think so? I just keep thinking…'

If anyone was to blame, it was him. He'd tried to reach the guy, put out the flames that had been licking around his sleeve, and he'd run. Maybe if he hadn't chased after him. Or if his knee had been stronger and he'd been able to catch him before he reached the road…

Now wasn't the time for those thoughts. He needed to focus on Abby, who seemed to be trying her damnedest to accept the blame that ought to be apportioned to him. 'I think that there was nothing more you could have done.'

She nodded. 'Why did he do it, Nick? I don't understand.'

'Fire-raising isn't the most logical of pursuits.' Nick wished he had a better answer for her. There was a time for thinking about motives and the sheer bloody waste of it all, and in his experience two o'clock in the morning wasn't it. 'Come along. You need to shower now, sweetheart.'

She looked up at him, gratitude in her eyes. 'Thanks for looking out for me, Nick.'

He shrugged. 'Forget it.' His own words seemed to stab at him, right between the ribs where his heart beat. 'No, on second thoughts, don't forget it.' He took her hands between his. 'I want you to remember, Abby, that you don't have to deal with everything alone. That there are people out there for you.'

She seemed just as much taken aback by what he'd said as he was at saying it. Nick gave them both a moment to digest it and then got to his feet. She took the hint and followed him to the bathroom.

'What about the woman who was driving the car? I thought I saw the police breathalysing her.'

Her mind was obviously still worrying at the loose ends from the evening, and if the truth was told there were plenty of them. 'Yep. They took her down to the police station. One of the guys told me that the breathalyser reading was positive.'

Abby slumped down into the chair in front of the mirror, staring at herself, as if the answers were there, written on her face. 'It all just seems so…so sad.'

'Yes. It is.' He made an effort to smile and even the watery result seemed to cheer her a little. 'But you said it yourself. We can't do everything, but we do our best. That has to be good enough.'

A tear rolled down her cheek. Nick watched it, realising that this was the first time he'd ever seen her cry. All she'd been through, and she'd saved the tears that might have been shed for herself to spend on a man who had tried to do her harm. Before he could do anything to comfort her, she had brushed it away.

'I don't suppose you noticed whether there was any hot chocolate left in the kitchen?'

Nick wasn't sure whether she really wanted hot chocolate, or whether she wanted to get rid of him. Or maybe she was just responding to his need to do something, anything, for her right now. Whatever. 'I'll go and see.'

When he returned, the sound of the shower running was filtering out from the bathroom. He put the Thermos mug down on the cabinet by the side of the bed, and then he heard it. The quiet sound of her weeping.

Abby wasn't sure why she had sent Nick away. Force of habit, she guessed. As she scrubbed at her body, cleaning away the blood that had soaked through the fabric of her jeans and the grime that streaked her arms and face, she half wished that he had ignored her and stayed.

You don't have to deal with everything alone. Nick had been there for her tonight. He'd known when to take charge and when to stand back and let her get on with what she had to do. Even then, she'd felt his strength.

The thought that it wasn't always going to be this way drove her to her knees, one hand over her mouth to silence the sounds of her tears. When she cried, she cried alone, always. And yet this time she wanted Nick to hold her.

She didn't hear the bathroom door open and she had no time to compose herself when he opened the shower door. There was no time to protest when he stepped inside, shutting off the flow of the water and lifting her to her feet and into his arms.

'It's okay, sweetheart.'

'It isn't, Nick. A man died.'

'That's not what I mean.' He caught a towel up, wrapping it around her shoulders, still keeping her body pressed safe against his. 'It's okay to feel afraid. To feel the pain when the odds are just too much against us, and we fail.'

Suddenly the dam broke. Abby reached for him, and hung on as tightly as she would have gripped a lifebelt thrown into stormy seas. Sobbing into his chest until she was breathless and gasping for air, then crying some more.

'That's it, sweetheart.' He seemed to understand that she wasn't just crying for tonight. That she was crying for all the other nights when she'd had no one to hold onto.

Finally the sobs subsided and embarrassment began to set in. 'Sorry.'

'Don't you dare.' He tilted her face up towards his, brushing her cheek with his thumb. 'We all cry, Abby. The best of us do it with a friend.'

She couldn't help a smile. Just a small one. 'You're all wet.'

'Mmm. So are you.' He wrapped the towel around her more firmly. 'We'll dry off, get into bed, and I'll hold you. Keep the wolves at bay.'

'Yours too?'

'Yep. Mine too. Tomorrow's a big day.'

'Today.' The thought of curling up with Nick soothed her. Maybe she would be able to sleep a little after all. 'It's today already.'

CHAPTER FOURTEEN

Day Six. Lake Windermere. Six long miles.

THE sky was an unbroken sheet of grey cloud, and the water was choppy in the stiff breeze. Today, of all days, the weather had decided to turn.

Her back ached. Her shoulders hurt from the efforts of last night out on the road, trying to save someone who could not be saved. Abby tried not to think about it. She could no longer help him, but there were other people she could help, if she did this swim.

Wading into the cold water, she swam for a while, up and down, getting used to the temperature and easing the aches in her body. She was swimming alone today. The small group of swimmers was on the jetty, ready to cheer her off and then drive to the finishing point. But Nick would be there. As he always was, on the boat, which was bobbing up and down by the starting point, ready to accompany her around the course.

'Okay, Abby?' She could see him waving and his voice drifted across the water. She struck out for the starting buoy.

Two miles. Already she was beginning to feel tired, and her shoulders were aching. It had been agreed that she would take feeds from the boat every two miles to help her keep her energy levels up, and Abby slowed, treading water as the boat closed in.

They were losing time, but it didn't matter. All that mattered was making the finish and she needed some nourishment today. Something to lift her spirits. Every time she'd started to get into a rhythm, the dull beat of a heart, which slowed and stopped, had echoed in her head.

Nick appeared at the side of the boat, leaning over so far that his shoulder was almost in the water. 'Here.' He handed her a warm drink and she took it from him, the brief almost-touch of his fingers more welcome than the drink.

'That's better.' She drank it down and threw the cup back onto the deck, behind him.

'Are your shoulders okay?' He was there again, this time handing her half a banana.

She hadn't said anything about her aches and pains, afraid that Nick wouldn't let her swim. He must have seen her easing her back and shoulders, though, before she'd got into the water. Noticed her erratic stroke.

'Yeah, fine. Just a little stiff.' She was feeling better already, although whether that was from the food and drink or the heat of his smile, she wasn't sure.

'Can you get a rhythm going?' He seemed to know exactly what the problem was.

'I'll try.' It was all she could promise.

'You have great rhythm.' His grin and the quick wink, which were just for her, were unmistakeable in their meaning. Abby flipped a few droplets of water towards him, and he laughed. 'Go for it, honey.'

She turned in the water, striking out away from the boat. Nick stayed by the side of the craft, his weight making it list slightly, signalling to Pete to stay in as close as possible. She could hear his voice, although it seemed miles away, calling out the beat of her strokes, and she focussed on that, trying to follow his lead.

Four miles. She was starting to flag again, and this time she reached a deeper pit than the last. The finish point looked about a hundred miles away and fatigue was thundering through her body, demanding that she give up. It had started to rain, and she could see almost nothing through her goggles, but she could feel the increasing choppiness of the water.

Nick again. Handing her a warm drink. Hazily she noticed that he was wearing a wetsuit, and wondered when he had put that on.

'Status, Abby.' His voice was warm, cajoling.

'My status is…shit.' Suddenly she couldn't go on. She wanted to be up in the boat. It wasn't the lake that had conquered her, it was everything else that had happened over the past few days.

'Sure it is.' She felt rather than saw his bulk sliding over the side of the boat and into the water. 'But you'll keep going.'

Damn him! She didn't want to keep going. She wanted to go back to the hotel and curl up somewhere warm and comfortable. But he was waving the boat away, and there was still a spark of something, deep down, that told her that she wasn't finished yet.

He started swimming and she followed him. Stroke for stroke. They swam together, Nick breathing to the right and Abby to the left so that they could see each other. One. Two. Then she saw his face in the water beside her. She kept going for that, ignoring the pain in her shoulders and back, living just to see his face one more time.

No words. No signals or glances. He was just there, swimming next to her. That meant more than anything. In a haze of determination and fatigue, her muscles screaming for respite, she just kept going, forgetting about anything other than the fact that he was there.

'Couple of hundred yards. Keep going.' His voice again. Was she really nearly there? Abby focussed in the direction she knew the finishing buoy must be, and saw it. Bobbing up and down in the water, and suddenly more beautiful than a buoy had any right to be.

She struck out for it, and then her fingers touched it. As they did so, she felt his arm around her in the water, supporting her. She held one aching arm up as a signal she'd touched home, and a cheer floated out across the water from the spectators lined up along the shoreline.

Exhilaration flooded through her. The boat was closing in, ready to pick them up, and she waved it away. 'I want to swim in.'

'That's my girl.' Nick was grinning broadly. Abby struck out for the shore and he followed, swimming with her until they were close enough in for their feet to touch the bottom.

He didn't touch her. Didn't help or support her as she struggled out of the water. She knew why. It had been her swim. He wasn't going to spoil that at the last minute. And even if she'd done six miles, and more, on plenty of occasions before, this one was different. She'd overcome so much more this time.

She fell to her hands and knees on the slippery

pebbles and he bent towards her. 'Stand up, Abby. You walk out, you don't crawl.'

His words jerked her to her feet. Just another couple of steps and she was clear of the water, and he had his arm around her waist, supporting her as her frozen, jelly-like legs made out that they were walking up the shingle. Letting her accept the wild delight of her welcoming committee for a few moments, he hustled her up to the windbreak that the team had erected by the side of a steep incline and guided her into its cover.

Numbly, she registered that he had her out of her wetsuit and costume and wrapped in a towel. Woolly hat, woollen socks and gloves to warm her frozen fingers. Warm trousers and a sweater then a jacket. It occurred to Abby that Nick had a talent for this. He'd got her out of her wetsuit and then raised her body temperature faster than seemed humanly possible.

'Thanks, Sam.' He acknowledged the mug that had suddenly appeared around the edge of the windbreak, the hand disappearing again in deference to the chance that one square inch of Abby's flesh might be exposed. 'What's so funny?'

'You.' She took the mug gratefully and took a sip. 'You're not as good at dressing me as undressing me. My jumper's on back to front.'

'Not so much practice. Or enthusiasm for the job.' He stripped off his wetsuit and grabbed the towel, winding it around his waist. 'I've got a change of clothes in the van.'

He'd come prepared. Known that she would be struggling this morning and had quietly gone about his own arrangements to support her, if she needed it. Gratitude warmed Abby's shivering limbs. Being there for her hadn't just been chance—he'd made sure of it, right from the start.

She followed him out of the cover of the windbreak, watching while he limped across the stony ground to the van. This had taken its toll on him as well.

A wolf whistle cut the air, making Abby jump. She'd turned her back on Nick and gone to accept the hugs and congratulations of the others while he opened the back of the van and got dressed. Abby imagined that no one was under any illusions about the nature of their relationship, but she didn't want to make it obvious by leering at him. She could look all she wanted later.

'What are you doing here, Lou?' His laughing voice was directed towards Sam's car, where Louise sat, wearing even more layers of clothing than Abby was.

'Enjoying the view, boss.' Louise wound down the window and leaned out. 'Wanna go through those moves again?'

Everyone laughed. Nick shook his head, buttoning his jeans and pulling a sweater over his head. After shave, again. Man runs out of water. Towels himself dry. Pulls sweater over perfectly muscled torso. Slowly. Nick was a real loss to the advertising industry.

Abby pushed those thoughts to the back of her head. Everyone else seemed to be taking the joke in good part, including Nick, who laughed at the barrage of comments from the crew, and disappeared into the back of the van, looking for his shoes. Limping back over towards her, he joined the group.

'Are you going to wait while we clear up and get the buoys in?' Sam turned to Abby. 'Or I can run you back to the hotel? I'm dropping Lou back there now. I just brought her out for half an hour to see the finish.'

'I'll stay.' Abby wanted to be with the team. Part of the jocular, no-holds-barred banter that they batted back and forth between them. Close to Nick, who was often the butt of their jokes but never seemed to retaliate beyond a slow shake of the head and a shrugging laugh. He was in charge, but never needed to show it. Teasing and jibes didn't seem so bad in this atmosphere.

Sam nodded and began to trudge across the shingle towards the car, leaving Abby to cajole Nick into sitting down with her in the shelter of the van. 'Where's your knee support?' She'd noticed that Nick had been moving gingerly across the rough ground.

'On the boat. The one I use for swimming is wet.' He grinned at her. 'It's okay.'

'Doesn't look it. Does it hurt?'

'Not really. I'm just tired. It gets weaker when I get tired. Perhaps you'll take a look at it when we get back to the hotel.'

He must be tired. But Abby knew he wouldn't

leave, any more than she would, until everything was packed up. She took the excuse of keeping warm and snuggled against him, watching as the boat drew up at the jetty and a couple of the men jumped aboard so they could help Pete haul the buoys in and bring them back to shore.

'I've been meaning to ask you.' Nick broke the silence.

'Ask away, then.'

She felt his chest heave as he took a breath. 'I know you were going to go home tomorrow. But the rest of us are staying here for another four days.'

'Yes?' Louise had already asked if she would stay over the weekend and Abby had already said yes. But she wanted Nick to ask. More than she had thought it was possible to want anything. Abby held her breath.

'So it would be great for Lou if you stayed. You could keep an eye on her.'

Disappointment curled around Abby's heart. 'Louise doesn't need me here.'

'No.'

'Right, then.' Maybe she would go home tomorrow after all.

'I do.'

She wanted to take the admission in her stride. Pretend that it didn't mean everything to her. It was just four days and then they'd go back to London and she would lose Nick again, for good. But it was four days of rest, relaxation and, if Abby had any say in the matter, more of that mind-blowing sex. Surely no one who could make love that way could be entirely unreachable. She was grasping at straws, and she knew it.

'Okay.'

'Yeah?' His grin said it all. The mind-blowing sex was a done deal.

'Yeah.' She smiled up at him. 'You only had to ask.'

The group of swimmers stayed together as a long, late lunch morphed into celebratory drinks at the bar and then into dinner. Abby made the effort to stay awake, but after dinner her fatigue began to overtake her again and she went to her room. Nick would join her later. The exchanged glance, his smile and the answering excitement in the pit of her stomach told her so.

She was dimly aware of him having been there during the night, but he hadn't woken her. Abby woke late, stretching her stiff limbs gingerly, to find that she was alone.

Nick must be up and around already. A stab of disappointment marred the dawning of what otherwise seemed to be a perfect day. Maybe he'd gone to get breakfast. Breakfast in bed would be nice.

As if responding to a cue, the doorhandle twisted silently and the door opened. Nick appeared, accompanied by the smell of coffee.

'Mmm. Just what I need this morning.'

'Thought you might.' He smiled at her and Abby's heart froze. He'd put the coffee down on the small writing desk in the corner of the room and sat upright on the hard-backed chair. His smile was nothing like the one he usually wore in the mornings.

'What's up?'

'Have some coffee.' He poured her a coffee and

handed it to her, leaving the other cup and the plate of croissants on the tray untouched.

'What's going on, Nick?'

'I have to leave.' He looked at his watch. 'In about fifteen minutes.'

'Why?' All Abby could think about were four words, playing and replaying in the back of head. *He said he'd stay.*

He planted his elbows on his knees, hands clasped tightly together. 'When I checked my emails first thing this morning there was one from yesterday, from the fire authority down in London. I've just called them, and they want to see me as soon as possible.'

'What about?' The look on his face told Abby that this couldn't be good.

'About the job offer they've made me. Seems that they were contacted yesterday by a national paper for a comment on the story that appeared in the newspaper here the other day.'

'What? But, Nick, I thought they already knew about your addiction. What on earth's going on?'

'They did…do…know. I was completely up-front with them. But this is a very public-facing job and it's a newly created post. Putting someone in who's just been disgraced in the papers might not be such a good idea. Politically speaking.'

Abby stared at him. 'So they're going to withdraw the job offer just because someone tells lies about you in the paper? That's not fair. I'm not entirely sure it's even legal.'

He shook his head abruptly. 'No, that's not the way it is, Abby. They just want to talk to me, about a little damage limitation. But if it's clear to me that taking up that job is going to hurt the service in any way, I'll be the first to pass on it. It's not just the story in the newspapers now. A man was killed the other night as well.'

'That wasn't your fault either. Nick, I know that this looks bad, but we can fight it. We can answer every single one of their questions and show them that you're not to blame for any of this.' Abby was pleading with him. Willing him to refocus. See things with the clarity with which she could see them.

A glimmer of gratitude showed in his eyes and it almost made Abby break down. Nick shouldn't need to be grateful for the truth. He was the most honourable man she knew, and this wasn't fair. 'We'll see.'

'Well, we have to tell them.' Abby put her cup and saucer down, and stood up. 'I'll be ready in ten minutes.'

He caught her arm. '*I* am going to tell them.'

'I was there, Nick. I saw what happened. Look, we don't have time to argue about this.'

'No, we don't.' He held her arm firmly. 'I'm going down to London to answer their questions. That's all it is, questions. No one's made a decision on anything yet.'

The look on his face made Abby shiver. 'What about you? Have you made a decision?'

'I won't be the one who brings the work of the fire service into disrepute. If I'm not going to be able to represent them properly, I'll step aside.'

'No. No, Nick, you can't do that. I won't let you. Surely the fire service won't let you.'

'They won't have any say in the matter. Neither do you.' His words were chilling enough. The look of grim determination on his face was even worse.

'Don't, Nick. Please don't...' Abby wondered whether tears would sway him. Probably not. They'd just make him feel worse about what he was going to do. She couldn't cry to order anyway.

His face softened. Maybe he knew that her heart was sobbing, screaming in pain. 'Abby, you can't stop me. Please, don't make this any more difficult than it already is. I have to go. Alone.'

'But... No, Nick, I'll go with you.'

'I said no.' The grim, lifeless look had recaptured his features. 'Abby, we were clear about this, right from the start. We were never going to keep things going between us when we got back to London. I sorry, but I have to go back now.' Abby knew what he was thinking. He'd been here once before, his job in jeopardy, the future uncertain. Nick was in damage-control mode. If they didn't have a relationship, then he couldn't ruin it.

He didn't wait for her answer. Abruptly he let go of her arm and he was out of the door before she could gather her wits, the scrape of a key sounding in the lock.

'Nick!' She beat against the door with her fists. 'Don't you dare…'

'Pete will come and let you out in half an hour when he gets back from the station. In the meantime, just simmer down, will you?'

Simmer down! She'd give him simmer down. Abby kicked the door hard, yelping as her bare toes impacted on the wood.

'Stop that. Just stay put and drink your coffee. This is for the best.'

'Okay. Okay, I'm calm now. There's no need to lock the door, I won't follow you.' Like hell she wouldn't. But raging wasn't going to make Nick open the door and she had to find a different tactic.

'Good. Sit tight, Abby.' A quiet bump on the other side of the door, the way the wood moved slightly against her cheek, told Abby that he was leaning against the door. Her fingers moved to where his cheek would be. Somehow she knew that it would be there, pressed against the door, just like hers was.

'Nick. I…' If she said it, she'd only scare him

away. If she didn't, she wouldn't get another chance.

'Me too, Abby. But it's time for us to wake up now. Go back to where we came from.' There was a sound, a movement on the other side of the door, and then silence. Abby listened for the sound of his footsteps, anything that meant she still had something left of him, but the carpet in the hallway robbed her of even that.

CHAPTER FIFTEEN

SHE contemplated sliding down to the floor, curling up in a ball and crying. Or screaming, beating her fists uselessly against the wood. She wanted to do both, but neither of those options was going to do any good. Abby took a deep breath and grabbed her phone.

'Louise, I need your help.' Abby cut short the lazy acknowledgement of her call, and explained quickly what had happened. She left out the bit about Nick having just walked away from everything that they had together and concentrating on the fact that he needed help and seemed determined not to take any.

'Okay. Are you dressed yet?'

'No, give me ten minutes, though, and I'll be ready.'

'Fine. You grab a shower and get dressed and I'll find Sam. Wait there for us.'

There wasn't much choice about that one, and

Louise had already cut the call anyway. Abby made for the bathroom, moving at speed.

Ten minutes later, almost to the second, there was a knock at the door. Abby lunged for the doorhandle, twisting it roughly.

'We can't find any spare keys in Reception, and Mrs P.'s disappeared off somewhere. But it's okay, Sam's coming for you. Can you open the window? Watch out for the ladder, and be careful you don't knock him off.'

Abby whirled round as a scraping sound at the window indicated that the ladder was being put into position. Muffled voices sounded outside, and she ran to the window, checked that Sam wasn't outside yet, and flung it open.

Sam was halfway up the ladder, a couple of his crewmates at the bottom holding it steady. It seemed that Nick had an all-out mutiny on his hands.

'Sam.' Right now she could have kissed him. 'Thank you.'

'Can you climb down?' Sam looked ready to throw her over his shoulder.

'Of course I can.'

'Right-oh.' Abby stumbled backwards as Sam levered his bulk through the window. 'Is your handbag and laptop all you need to bring?'

'Yes. I don't have time to pack. Can I give you a ring later about my things?'

'Sure thing. You climb down first, and I'll follow.' He gave a wave to the men below, and helped Abby out of the window, making sure her hands and feet were securely on the ladder. 'Don't rush, there's plenty of time. Move one hand or one foot at a time.'

Abby grinned at him and began to climb down. The ladder was rock steady, held both at the bottom and by Sam at the top. She made the ground, and Sam followed quickly, her bags thrown over his shoulder.

Louise appeared, walking briskly around the corner of the building, bundled up in a fleecy jacket. 'Let's get a move on, then.' She was obviously in charge of this particular operation. 'Come on, Sam, we don't have any time to waste.'

Nick walked into the steel and glass reception area. It was almost deserted, apart from the receptionist, who was talking intently to a young woman who had her back to him. A blonde, corn-coloured plait, which fell down her back made his stomach lurch uncomfortably. Today every-one looked like Abby.

He'd done the right thing. It had almost ripped his heart from his chest to leave Abby behind like that, but this wasn't her battle. And somehow he'd managed to overcome the almost unstoppable urge to let her help him fight it. It was enough to know that she'd wanted to. He needed to let her go now, while he was still strong enough to do so. Before he descended into the chaos that now seemed to await him.

The woman at the reception desk turned and he almost dropped his briefcase. She was dressed in a fitted red jacket, with a black skirt and high heels. Carrying a leather notecase under her arm. Looking more alluring than any woman had a right to look. Abby.

Abby. How had she got here? She'd been locked in her room. Pete had been instructed not to let her out until he got back from the station, and then only if she promised not to leave the premises. There was only one other train that could have got her here in time, the one that had left an hour after the one he had taken.

It was impossible. Just as the red of her lips was impossible. The silky sheen of her stockings and the way that the light glinted in her fair hair. She was businesslike, sexy and completely gorgeous, all at the same time. No man in his right mind could resist her.

'What the hell are you doing here?' He took her by the elbow and muttered the words into her ear.

'Ah, here he is.' Abby turned to the receptionist with a smile.

The receptionist nodded. 'I'll call and let them know you're here, Mr Hunter. It'll be a few minutes as you're early, so please take a seat.'

'Thank you.' Nick managed a smile and almost frog-marched Abby over to the group of chairs furthest from the reception desk. He waited for her to sit down and pulled one of the leather chairs up close to her seat. 'I repeat, Abby, what the hell are you doing here?'

'I came to give you something.' She was as brittle as a dry stick, holding herself tense and straight. He wanted to hold her, have her melt into his arms. He wanted to get her out of here, so that he could do what he had to do.

'What?'

'This.' She opened the briefcase and drew out a folder, laying it front of him. Nick stared at it. 'This is my account of what happened the night before last. I wrote it on the train on the way down from Cumbria. There are accounts from all of the crew, as well as statements about their confidence in you. They emailed them through to me and I printed them out when I got home.' She gave a little smile. 'While I was changing into my battle gear.' She knew how good she looked. She'd done it deliberately, so that no one would question her right to be here. So that he wouldn't send her away.

'Abby.' He longed to pick the folder up, take hold of what she was offering him. With an effort of will he kept his hands still, fingers gripping the arms of his chair. 'It doesn't make any difference. It's not a matter of the way things are, it's how they look. The people I'm meeting know what happened. They don't need to see this.'

'Well, that's fine, because it's not for them. It's for you.'

'I can't do this, Abby. I can't put my own interests above those of the fire service.'

'No one's asking you to. If you believed in yourself as much as the people who work for you do, you'd know that staying and fighting was the best thing for you and the service. That you've got far too much to give to just turn and walk away.' She reached forward and twitched at the cover of the folder and it fell open. 'Read any page, Nick. They all say the same.'

'Don't, Abby.' She was picking away at the whole fabric of his being. Everything that he believed in. He didn't have time for this now, he'd already made his decision about how he was going to handle this meeting.

'It's done, Nick. I'm here. This folder's here. You can turn your back on all of it if you like, but you'll be doing a gross disservice to the fire service and to yourself.' Her lip was quivering.

'Mr Hunter…Nick Hunter.' The receptionist's voice drifted across the cavernous space. 'You can go up now.'

'Can you give me one minute, please?' The receptionist nodded and Nick turned back to face Abby.

'Just take it, Nick. Put it in your briefcase.' She pushed the folder towards him with shaking fingers. 'You don't need to read it. It's enough to know what's there, inside it.'

Maybe it was. If only he had more time. Half an hour, fifteen minutes even. Nick picked up the folder and stowed it safely away in his case. 'Abby...I...'

'Go, Nick.' She summoned a smile. 'Good luck. Make the right decision.'

He couldn't bear to look at her any more. Couldn't stand to even think about what she was offering him. It would kill him if he started to believe that he could be the man he wanted to be, and then had those illusions shattered. Better stay with what he knew. He nodded in her direction, hardly even looking at her, then turned and walked away.

Abby had accepted coffee from the young woman at the reception desk. She'd read the leaflets stacked in the display rack and done a mental fire-safety audit on her flat. Twenty questions, eighteen of which she could answer satisfactorily. If nothing else came out of today, at least she would make sure to test her smoke alarms regularly in future.

She'd done what she'd come to do, but she couldn't leave. Maybe Nick would need someone to speak up for him in the meeting. Someone who had been there, and who could refute any of the claims that the papers might be making.

'They won't be long now.' The receptionist gave her a smile. She could hardly have missed Abby's agitation, the way that she had been hard put to sit still for the last hour and a half. 'You'll be able to see when they come out.'

'Where?' Abby scanned the large, double-storey reception space. A maze of glass and steel, which gave the impression that the building was transparent, without it actually being so.

'Up there.' The receptionist pointed to a mirror set above the entrance doors. 'You can see the entrance to the conference room.' The mirror was angled so that the area next to the lifts was clearly visible from the reception desk. 'It's handy for me to keep an eye on what's going on down here and up there at the same time, without getting whiplash.'

Abby grinned, staring up at the mirror. As if in response to the intensity of her gaze, the conference-room door opened. 'Look. Is that them?'

'Yeah. Looks as if it's gone well.'

It did. Nick was standing with three other uniformed officers, and all four were talking. Laughing. Nick seemed taller somehow, his body language quite different from when he had walked away from her. As if a weight had been lifted from his shoulders.

'Do you think so?' Abby needed a second opinion. This was too important to believe the evidence of her own eyes.

'Commander Evans is staying to talk. That's always a sign that he's happy with the way things have gone. Your friend should be too.' The receptionist gave her an encouraging nod and it occurred to Abby that she probably knew exactly what this meeting was about, along with everything else that went on in the building. Abby looked upwards again and saw Nick shaking hands warmly with what seemed to be the senior man. This was no polite *sorry it didn't work out* handshake.

'He'll be down in a minute.' The receptionist was looking at her intently, and Abby realised that she had tears in her eyes.

'Yes. Look, I have to go. Will you tell him... tell him I said good luck.'

'But he won't be a moment.'

'Yes. Yes, I know. Will you tell him, please?' Abby knew all she needed to know. Nick had taken the step. He'd believed in himself, and he'd fought for his future. Louise would let her know the details, all in good time. For now this was everything. And she wasn't going to spoil it by hearing Nick's goodbye. She'd heard that once today and it had broken her heart. She knew just how much she was capable of, and what was coming next was way beyond that.

'Sure.' The receptionist shrugged.

'It's important.'

'I'll tell him. No one gets in or out of this building without me knowing about it.'

'Thanks. I appreciate it. Really appreciate it.' Abby turned and almost ran out of the building, her high heels echoing on the granite floor. Harsh. Lonely. She was going to have to get used to that.

CHAPTER SIXTEEN

ABBY smoothed her hair and took a final twirl in front of the mirror. She looked fine. A little gaunt maybe, but she hadn't been eating. She hadn't been sleeping much either, but twenty minutes in front of the mirror had taken care of the dark circles under her eyes.

Her first instinct had been to rip up the crisp, white card that had arrived in the post, begging the pleasure of her company on Saturday evening at a party to be held in celebration of the success of the swim. She didn't want to see Nick again. He'd turned out to be the one man that she'd been looking for. The one she could trust. The one she could love. She'd been so afraid that he might break her heart, but Abby had gone ahead and done that all on her own, by wanting things that Nick had told her he couldn't give.

But Louise had called, begging her to come,

then Pete and then finally Sam, who sounded as if he was reading from a prepared script and who awkwardly used all the entreaties that Louise had already fired at her, and in addition just happened to mention that Nick wouldn't be there, because he was out of town on a trip in connection with his new job. Abby had put him out of his embarrassed misery and accepted. It would be good to see everyone again.

The doorbell went at exactly six-thirty. Opening the living-room window, Abby saw Louise at the main door to her block of flats and waved down to her, before picking up her handbag and the soft woollen wrap she'd chosen in case the evening became chilly and going downstairs.

'Hey, you look nice! Give me a twirl!' Louise squealed her approval as Abby spun round, the red, filmy skirt of her dress floating out around her legs.

'You look lovely, too.' If the last three weeks had taken their toll on Abby, they'd obviously been kind to Louise. She'd lost the deep hollows under her eyes and was healthy and beaming.

'Are you sure we're not a bit overdressed for the fire station?'

'No, I said to wear something nice. And it's not exactly the fire station. There's some land at the back, adjoining the park. We use it to park the truck on when we have open days.'

'Oh.' That didn't sound much like somewhere you'd dress up for either, but Louise seemed to know what she was doing, and Abby obediently got into the car when Sam jumped out to open the door for her.

Everything became clear when Sam drew up outside the fire station, letting the women out and driving away to find a parking place. Louise led Abby along an alleyway to the side of the main buildings, which opened up into a large courtyard at the back, walls on three sides to separate it completely from the working area, the fourth side open to the empty parkland beyond and cordoned off with ropes. There was a marquee, and the trees that surrounded it were decorated with lights, which were just beginning to sparkle as dusk approached.

'See. Looks pretty, doesn't it.'

'It's beautiful. I never would have imagined that this was here. Who did all this?'

'Oh, some of the guys.' Louise was walking briskly, almost dragging Abby behind her. She slowed when she got near the marquee, opening the flap and motioning Abby inside.

The tent was ablaze with light, a temporary floor laid on the uneven ground, tables along one side for food and drink and soft music coming from speakers slung in the canopy. And it was completely empty. Abby whirled around to find Louise, only to see that she had disappeared.

'Hey, Abby.'

Light suddenly dawned. Abby took a deep breath to steady herself, and turned round slowly to face Nick.

He looked fantastic. A crisp, white shirt, open at the neck, with a dark suit. It didn't take much to make Nick look delicious. In fact, it didn't take anything at all.

'I think I've been set up.' She took one cautious step towards him. Another self was screaming at her to turn and run, get out of there, but she ignored it. Her heart was already shattered into little pieces. What more could he do to her?

'Yes, you have.' His body language was tense, like a coiled spring, but his dark eyes were full of tenderness and he was smiling. He seemed happy to see her.

'So there's no party?'

'It starts at eight.' He shrugged. 'And I am, as you can see, here. I have to be really, it's my party. Something to say thank you to everyone.'

'You did all this?'

'Yes.'

They'd run out of things to say already. Suddenly Abby didn't want any more of this. She turned away from him, but he was at her side in one swift movement, his hand laid gently on her arm. 'Don't go, Abby. Please.' A pulse beat at the side of his jaw.

'There's nothing more to say.' She was close to tears. 'I don't know why you went to such lengths to get me here, Nick. Nothing's changed. We said that we wouldn't carry on with things after we got back to London, and we haven't.'

'I have something to say. And since you won't

take my calls, I had to resort to subterfuge. Did you listen to any of my messages?'

'No.'

'Didn't think so.' Her admission had hurt him, however much he seemed to have expected it. She could see her own anguish reflected in his eyes.

'What's the point, Nick?' Abby was trying to be angry with him but she couldn't. All she felt was grief, tearing at her.

'I just want a minute of your time, Abby. Just one minute, to say what I want to say, and then you can do whatever you want. I'll take you home if you want to go, or you can stay here until the party starts.' His gaze left her face, slipping downwards to the floor between them. 'If you want me to beg, that's fine. I can do that for you, Abby.'

She took pity on him. 'One minute. And then I'll ask Sam to take me home.'

'Yeah. If that's what you want I'll go and fetch him. In a minute.'

'That's what I want.' Why couldn't he have left things alone? 'What is it you have to say?'

'I've been thinking hard about this, Abby.' He hesitated. 'Won't you come and sit down with me?'

'No. It's okay, go on.' Sitting down was unnecessary. And he'd already wasted five seconds of the time she'd promised him.

'I'm not afraid any more, Abby. I can have a cup of coffee in the morning or go for a beer after work, without feeling that it's the first step on a slippery slope that's going to lead to addiction. I'm not my father and I never will be.'

'I know that, Nick. You proved it, when you believed in yourself and fought to keep your job.'

Some of the tension left his face, and the suspicion of a grin threatened the corners of his mouth. 'You believed in me, Abby. You gave me the chance to be the man that I want to be. With you by my side I could have faced anything— a shattered knee, a broken career—and still not given up. I know I've made mistakes in the past, and that I don't deserve you, but I do love you and I want more than anything to make you happy.'

'What?' Abby caught her breath so quickly that she started to choke. His arm shot around her waist and he led her to a chair, sitting her down and fetching her a glass of water.

'Here. Are you all right?'

Abby flapped her hand impatiently at him. 'No. Not really.' She took a few sips of the water.

'Heimlich?'

'Don't you dare.'

'Tissue?' He reached for his pocket.

'No, thanks.' She didn't care about the tears that were streaming down her face. 'Nick, are you quite mad?'

'Don't think so. Although you're the medic, so I guess you'd be better placed to make a call on that than me.'

'But you said…you said you didn't want…'

'I know. I was a fool.' He pulled a chair over and sat down opposite her, leaning forward, his elbows on his knees. 'You're the best thing that ever happened to me, Abby. And we're good together, can't you feel that?'

She felt it. Abby reached out, letting her fingertips graze his cheek. How she'd longed to touch him again. A shiver ran through his frame, and he grasped her hand, holding it for one more precious moment against his skin. 'I'm afraid, Nick.'

'That's okay, Abby. It's okay to be afraid but please trust me. You were there when I needed you, let me be here for you now.'

'I do trust you, Nick.' Maybe, just maybe he could achieve the impossible and make this right.

'I won't ruin this chance by leaving you in any doubt about how I feel. I love you. I want to marry you. I want us to live together and have children. I want you to never stop telling me when you think I'm in the wrong, because I trust your judgement better than I do my own.' He pursed his lips. 'Mostly.'

'Mostly!'

'Well, no one's right one hundred per cent of the time. But you were right about me. You saw me for what I was, made me change, and the man you changed me into fell in love with you. Then you left.'

'I thought…'

'I know what you thought, Abby. You thought that I was strong enough to stick to what I said about splitting up with you when we left Cumbria. You overestimated me there.'

'Maybe I underestimated you. Maybe I underestimated myself. I didn't think that either of us could change.' She smiled at him and he caught his breath, his face reflecting her own hope.

'But we could. We did. Giving in to you, Abby, was the best thing I ever did.'

'You put up a fight, though.'

'So did you. I loved every moment of it. We're both fighters, Abby, but there's no malice there, we fight because we care. Then we make up.' He leaned forward and kissed her forehead lightly. 'I particularly love that part of it.'

'Yes. Me too.' That sweet surrender. His and hers, together. 'I…I suppose we could buy a house. Or live in yours. My flat's not really big enough.' Tentatively she began to allow her imagination to explore everything he'd offered her. All the delights.

'We'll find somewhere that we both fall in love with. Somewhere that's big enough for the family we'll make together.'

His face was alive with possibilities. Dreams

that Abby thought she'd dreamt alone. 'I'd like that, Nick. A family. You'd make a great father.'

'We can get started on that just as soon as you'd like.' A hint of mischief glinted in his eyes. 'I'll always love you, Abby. And I'll always do my best to protect you and make you happy.'

It was all or nothing now. She was going to try for it all. 'I'll always love you too, Nick. You've already made me happy.'

He fell suddenly to one knee in front of her, taking her hands in his. 'Will you marry me, Abby?'

'Yes, I will.' She answered the question as swiftly as it was asked. Why delay? She didn't need to think about it, she knew it was what she wanted, and she couldn't wait a moment longer.

They were both grinning like children, hardly ready to believe what they'd just done. Finally Nick seemed to remember something and felt in his pocket. 'I've got a ring. If you don't like it…'

'I don't think there's much chance of that.' If he tied a piece of string around her finger it would be the most precious thing in the world to her.

Abby held out her hand, noticing that it was trembling, almost as if it didn't belong to her.

'We'll see. Close your eyes.' She felt his hands on hers and a little thrill of anticipation coursed through her as his lips brushed her cheek. Then she felt him slip the ring onto her finger.

'It's beautiful, Nick.'

'You haven't opened your eyes yet.'

'Yes, I know. It's beautiful.'

He laughed and then he kissed her. Soft, tender, with that delicious edge of longing that told her that there was more. That there would always be more. She clung to him, and he held her tight.

'Open your eyes, sweetheart. Please. Make it real.'

Abby opened her eyes, staring up at his face. Then she looked at the ring on her finger. A gold band, with a fire opal flanked by two diamonds.

She caught her breath. 'It's…it's the most precious thing I've ever owned, Nick.'

'I wanted to have something to give you if you said yes. But if it's not what you want, we can change it…'

'I love it. It's beautiful.' She wrapped her right

hand protectively over the fingers of her left, hugging them to her chest. 'Don't you dare try and take it back.'

He chuckled, all assurance again. 'I won't take it back.' He took her hands in his, kissing her fingers. 'Would you like to dance? Or I have a crate of champagne stowed under the table if you'd like something to drink.'

'Yeah? Pretty sure of yourself, weren't you?'

He laughed. 'Not really. I was going to save it for the next try if you said no.'

'There was going to be a next try?'

'You don't imagine I was going to give up, do you?'

Abby laughed. 'Now you come to mention it, no, I don't. Thanks.'

'What for?'

'Not giving up on me.'

'I'll never give up on you, sweetheart. Dance with me.'

It was five to eight and Louise and Sam had drunk more than enough tea with the crew on duty in the ready room. Nick still hadn't phoned, as agreed, to let Louise know the coast was clear.

'Perhaps she's killed him.'

'Nah. Nick knows when to duck.' Sam grimaced.

'We'd better go and see. Before everyone else starts to arrive.' Timekeeping was a habit. The tent would start filling up at the stroke of eight.

Louise hurried downstairs and across the uneven ground to the marquee, Sam in tow, along with Pete and his wife, whom they'd met on the way. Carefully twitching at the tent flap and peering inside, she flung it open, laughing delightedly. Nick and Abby were together, on the dance floor, swaying in perfect time to the slow beat of the music, as if they were the only two people in the world.

Nick looked up, his face shining. 'What are you waiting for? Help yourself to champagne. I'm—'

'Engaged.' Abby was glowing too. 'We're both engaged right now.'

* * * * *

Mills & Boon® Large Print Medical

May

MAYBE THIS CHRISTMAS...?	Alison Roberts
A DOCTOR, A FLING & A WEDDING RING	Fiona McArthur
DR CHANDLER'S SLEEPING BEAUTY	Melanie Milburne
HER CHRISTMAS EVE DIAMOND	Scarlet Wilson
NEWBORN BABY FOR CHRISTMAS	Fiona Lowe
THE WAR HERO'S LOCKED-AWAY HEART	Louisa George

June

FROM CHRISTMAS TO ETERNITY	Caroline Anderson
HER LITTLE SPANISH SECRET	Laura Iding
CHRISTMAS WITH DR DELICIOUS	Sue MacKay
ONE NIGHT THAT CHANGED EVERYTHING	Tina Beckett
CHRISTMAS WHERE SHE BELONGS	Meredith Webber
HIS BRIDE IN PARADISE	Joanna Neil

July

THE SURGEON'S DOORSTEP BABY	Marion Lennox
DARE SHE DREAM OF FOREVER?	Lucy Clark
CRAVING HER SOLDIER'S TOUCH	Wendy S. Marcus
SECRETS OF A SHY SOCIALITE	Wendy S. Marcus
BREAKING THE PLAYBOY'S RULES	Emily Forbes
HOT-SHOT DOC COMES TO TOWN	Susan Carlisle

Mills & Boon® Large Print
Medical

August

THE BROODING DOC'S REDEMPTION — Kate Hardy
AN INESCAPABLE TEMPTATION — Scarlet Wilson
REVEALING THE REAL DR ROBINSON — Dianne Drake
THE REBEL AND MISS JONES — Annie Claydon
THE SON THAT CHANGED HIS LIFE — Jennifer Taylor
SWALLOWBROOK'S WEDDING OF THE YEAR — Abigail Gordon

September

NYC ANGELS: REDEEMING THE PLAYBOY — Carol Marinelli
NYC ANGELS: HEIRESS'S BABY SCANDAL — Janice Lynn
ST PIRAN'S: THE WEDDING! — Alison Roberts
SYDNEY HARBOUR HOSPITAL: EVIE'S BOMBSHELL — Amy Andrews
THE PRINCE WHO CHARMED HER — Fiona McArthur
HIS HIDDEN AMERICAN BEAUTY — Connie Cox

October

NYC ANGELS: UNMASKING DR SERIOUS — Laura Iding
NYC ANGELS: THE WALLFLOWER'S SECRET — Susan Carlisle
CINDERELLA OF HARLEY STREET — Anne Fraser
YOU, ME AND A FAMILY — Sue MacKay
THEIR MOST FORBIDDEN FLING — Melanie Milburne
THE LAST DOCTOR SHE SHOULD EVER DATE — Louisa George

MRV   COA

Return to . . . .
or any other Aber
Please return/renev
by phone or online

3 0 JUL :

0 6 SEP 2

Co 5)·5

SW 2/16

2 9

X000 000 047 4632

ABERDEEN CITY LIBRARIES